JEB STRAUSS AND GRANT'S GOLD

JOHN V. SUTER

LAAGER MOUNTAIN PRESS

ISBN-13: 978-8-218-12871-5

Cover design by: Jeffrey Dooley and Lauren Grant
Printed in the United States of America

For Rebecca.
Your light never fades.

CHAPTER 1

Where is Porter's Flat

The sun sets behind the misty peaks and tall pine trees along the banks of Webb Creek. The landscape is closed as the rhododendron creeps to the edge of the bank. The water rushes through the channel, and it spills over the large rocks strewn from the peaks into the watery current. Most creek beds look similar in the mountains of east Tennessee, and today, with daylight fading, the darkness envelops this valley quickly.

Jeb Strauss sits on a flat slab of sandstone at the edge of the cascading water. The sound of the water striking the exposed sides of the boulders creates a roar in the otherwise quiet forest. Jeb pushes his wide-brim river hat back to the top of his head and removes his thick black-rimmed glasses, wiping away bits of water with the sleeve of his shirt. He carefully places his glasses on his nose and scans the shallow portions of the creek along the rocky bank.

"Hey!"

Jeb turns, and Clem Clements, a short, round man with red sideburns, waddles through the small pools of water. His round face is red, and he is breathing heavily. "You said you would wait on me!" he bellows, standing in a slow-flowing pool of clear water.

"I *am* waiting for you," Jeb says with a smile, "right here on this rock." Jeb slaps the stone with his hand and sends an echo through the small ravine. "Get up here," Jeb continues. "We don't have much light left."

"You said we would be out of here before dark," Clem bristles.

"Nobody has ever followed Perry Shults's trail this far into the mountains," Jeb says defensively.

"And we still aren't there yet," Clem grumbles.

"Patience. You just need a little patience." Jeb laughs. "The entrance to Shults's gold mine is around here. I can feel it. I can smell the gold in the air."

"I don't smell anything but pine trees and the fishy water I'm standing in."

Jeb takes a rolled piece of brown paper from his pack and unfurls it. He studies the red lines he has drawn that correspond to the creek he is standing beside. He scans the horizon, but the thickness of the trees and underbrush limit the distance.

"Do you think it is in there?" Clem says

breathlessly as he climbs the boulder where Jeb is standing.

"Yep," Jeb says distantly as he looks from the forest to the map.

"And there are gold and silver coins in it?"

"Exactly," Jeb says with a smile.

His blue eyes dance as he grabs Clem by the hand and pulls him on top of the rock. "Our aerial survey was very fruitful. It led us up this steep gorge to this point, and I believe we are near the lost Shults Mine entrance. The Perry Shults mine is a prize of East Tennessee legend."

Perry Shults was a blacksmith in the 1860s who operated a mine in the mountains of East Tennessee. He ran the mine for years until his death. Unfortunately for his family, he never told anyone where the mine was located. The mine entrance has been hidden for over a hundred years.

"I don't know, Jeb," Clem says, struggling to his feet, "it is just a story."

"It is real," Jeb says with a grin. Jeb reaches into his pocket and extracts a shiny silver coin.

Clem's eyes gleam greedily as he stares at the shimmering coin.

"This is why we conducted the aerial magnetic survey from your plane," Jeb says with a smile. "This is why we did the lidar survey with the drone. This, my friend, is the proof that what we are doing will pay off."

Clem licks his lips greedily and reaches his trembling hand toward the fat silver coin. Jeb flips the coin in the air, and Clem's eyes follow the coin upward as it rotates in the air. Jeb jabs his hand into the air, snatching the coin. He laughs, thrusting the coin into his pocket. Clem intently watches Jeb's pocket with his mouth agape. "Now we just need to find the entrance to the mine," Jeb says as he scans the shoreline.

"We're camping out here tonight?" Clem says as he looks from the stream to the thick forest.

The gurgling water seems to grow softer as the darkness spreads in the river gorge. A whip-poor-will sings in the distance, and the forest comes alive as the treefrogs begin their serenade. Jeb studies the map. He has drawn lines on the page that correlate to the magnetic survey. He squints his eyes as he brings the map closer to his face. He shakes his head and quickly extracts his tactical flashlight from his pack.

The gorge is shrouded in shadow, and a cool breeze blows through the channel from the angular peaks above. *Thunk.*

Clem grabs Jeb's shoulder. "What was that?"

Jeb shrugs his shoulders, and Clem grips his shirt forcefully.

Thunk. Splash!

"There is something out there," Clem whispers.

Jeb shines the bright-blue beam from his flashlight along the edge of the creek.

"Man, this place gives me the creeps," Clem says softly, looking into the thick undergrowth.

Jeb steps to the edge of the boulder, passing the beam from the flashlight across the surface of the water. He listens carefully for another sound, but nothing happens. "Probably a frog hitting the water," Jeb says as he passes the beam across the surface again. A sparkle of light flashes in the path of the flashlight. Jeb stops and passes the beam back across the water, and the sparkle reappears. Jeb jumps off the boulder into a shallow pool below.

Jeb wades slowly through the flowing water, scanning the bottom of the creek. A twinkling light reflects faintly from the bottom as the flashlight beams strikes its surface. Jeb carefully steps on the slick rocks and positions his feet firmly on a large, stable stone. He slowly dips his hand into the cold mountain water and touches the radiating object at the bottom.

His breath catches in his throat as he extracts the relic from the pool. Jeb bites his lip as he stares at the gold coin. "Oh my," he whispers as he runs his fingers across the surface. He places the coin between his teeth and bites the surface. He holds the coin in the light, and his teeth marks are visible. "Extraordinary," Jeb says with a smile. He searches the surrounding pools with the light as he walks slowly upstream. Jeb climbs two, then three larger rocks, and the beam of light strikes the surface of the water, causing another sparkle.

Another coin. Jeb extracts the gold from its rocky bed and holds it in the beam from the flashlight. He is close. Really close. *Splash!*

Jeb turns toward the sound, and Clem is scrambling to his feet with water dripping from his clothes. "What do you have there?" Clem says excitedly as he shakes his legs, sending droplets of water in all directions.

"Proof," Jeb says with a wide smile.

Jeb flips the coin toward Clem. Clem catches the coin, and his eyes shine as he stares at the gold. "It *is* real," Clem says breathlessly.

"And it is somewhere around here," Jeb says, scanning the riverbank with the flashlight.

"How did this get in the creek?"

"Washed out of the mine by rainwater and deposited here," Jeb replies slowly.

"Is it over there where you're looking?" Clem says licking his lips.

Jeb removes his tablet from his pack and opens the lidar survey. The screen is filled with orange, yellow, and green colors. The survey shows normal mountain terrain with angular blocks of stone and slabs of rock. The lidar data also shows a rectangular structure somewhere on the north side of the creek.

"I don't see anything!" Clem bellows.

Jeb cuts his eyes in Clem's direction and thrusts his finger onto the rectangular pattern on the screen. "This is manmade," Jeb says confidently.

"How do you know? It looks like all the other lines," Clem replies impatiently.

"All the other forms are angular, but this has perfectly square corners."

"So?" Clem bristles.

"So, perfect square corners means somebody carved it," Jeb says with a nod.

"Oh. We are looking for that then?"

"That is the honey hole," Jeb says as he places the tablet carefully in his pack. He slings it onto his back, then sloshes through the current toward the north bank of the river.

"Wait up! Wait up! You're not finding it without me," Clem says as he splashes through the cold, shallow water.

The trees along the rocky bank bend as the cool breeze blows across the water. Jeb's pantlegs stick to his skin as he climbs the sandstone blocks along the creek. The wet fabric grips the surface of the rock, slowing his progress. Jeb pulls his legs forcefully toward the summit, and the knees of his pants rip open. "Ah man," he says as he stands upright.

Jeb shines the flashlight into the rhododendron that is growing thickly along the edge of the waterway. The beam of blue light is the only light visible, as darkness has enveloped the river valley.

"Any luck?" Clem says, out of breath behind him.

"Should be on the other side of these trees," Jeb says, studying the terrain. He jumps from the boulder and climbs through the thick vegetation. The branches snag and tear at his clothes and skin as he moves between their trunks.

"I can't get through this, Jeb," Clem grumbles.

"Crawl, then," Jeb barks as a branch swipes his face. A bead of blood trickles slowly down Jeb's cheek as he pushes through the last layers of growth. Jeb stands in a pine and oak forest with a mix of leaves and pine needles strewn on the ground. There are vertical rock faces positioned in between the towering trees. They form ascending layers that reach upward toward the top of the mountain.

Jeb walks slowly along the edge of a limestone wall, searching the rocks for an opening. His steps are muffled by the decaying needles. He shines the light ahead of him, and a four-foot-tall rectangular formation greets his eyes. "Oh yeah," he whispers. At the base of the rock wall is a carved rectangular wall with a series of steps leading into the shear rock cliff. As he looks at the formation, he realizes it does look natural. The steps look like the stones protrude from the ground. "This is why no one ever found this place. It was hidden in plain sight," Jeb says.

"What are you talking about?" Clem grumbles.

Jeb turns, and Clem is crawling on the ground through the thick undergrowth. "You need some help?" Jeb says, laughing.

"You could have helped me with the flashlight," Clem replies with a huff. "These branches took part of my hide with them."

Jeb shines the light on the entrance to the Shults mine. Clem stands beside Jeb, looking at the lit rock face. "What are we looking at?" Clem asks.

"This is it," Jeb says as he starts toward the

stairs.

"It's just rocks," Clem replies, hurrying after.

Jeb stands at the wall and passes the blue beam from the flashlight into the darkness. The steps are broken and have shifted upward, making the entrance look like a natural cave formation. "See? It's a cave—nothing else," Clem grumbles.

Jeb shakes his head as a flicker of light comes from between two sunken slabs on the ground. Jeb hops onto the uneven rocks and shines the blue beam into the crevice. He delicately extracts a shiny silver coin and holds it in the blue light. "You wanted proof, and this is it," Jeb says, eyeing the silver medallion.

Clem rushes down the stone slabs chaotically into the darkness below. Jeb scans the depths of the mine with the bright light. The entrance descends at a thirty-degree angle for about twenty yards, and then the pathway flattens. Clem's enormous body disrupts the illumination of the mineshaft. Jeb narrows his eyes and shakes his head. "Why do I always bring him?" he mutters.

At the base of the makeshift stairs, Clem is standing with wide eyes and mouth hanging open, hypnotized. Jeb walks around his large frame, and there at his feet are ten wooden crates. In the pale-blue glow of the tunnel, the shimmering silver coins spill from the old, worn compartments. "H-how m-much you think is in th-there?" Clem stutters.

Rocks rain down on Jeb and Clem. Jeb covers his head and hurries deeper into the tunnel. Clem stumbles over one of the crates and falls with a *thud*. Rocks the size of baseballs pummel his body. Clem's screams fill the mineshaft as he struggles to his feet. Jeb hears a faint tapping, like metal on solid stone, coming from the mine entrance. He flips the flashlight off, and they are shrouded in a thick darkness. Small pebbles trickle down the stone steps, and Jeb can feel a slight vibration in the floor. "Over here," Jeb whispers.

Clem grunts loudly, and a few seconds later, he is breathing heavily beside Jeb. "What's going on?" Clem says through is clenched teeth.

"We were about to ask you the same thing," a voice says in the darkness.

CHAPTER 2

Silver and Gold

A bright-red light erupts beside Jeb showering him with sparks that singe the hairs on his arms. Jeb grabs Clem by the shoulder and drags him deeper into the cave, away from the bright burning stick.

"Don't leave so soon," a tall, wiry man with long gray hair says is a raspy voice. He is standing at the top of the stairs, and he slowly descends into the mine as the flare fizzles. "Seems to me you boys done found yourselves in somebody's house. And in these parts, thieves are treated most unkindly," he says with a grin.

"We didn't see anything!" Jeb yells.

"I think they've seen everything, Joe," says a hulking man with tattoo sleeves on both arms.

"No need for our new friends to know who we are," Joe says, shaking his head.

"Right," says the henchman.

Joe sits on the wooden crates and pulls a

Bowie knife from his belt, holding it so Clem and Jeb can see it. The red flare glints off the polished silver surface. Joe scratches his neck with the blade as he eyes Jeb suspiciously. The sound of steel scraping against stubble fills the mineshaft. Jeb looks at the henchman behind him and Joe seated in front of him. The only routes out of this mess are gone.

"Like I said before, we didn't see anything. We were hiking and found this place. What is it exactly?"

Joe laughs loudly, and his whole body shakes. "Now that's the funniest thing I've ever heard," Joe says between laughs. Instantly, he stops and looks at them through narrow eyes. "We've been watching you boys since you ventured up our creek."

"We were hiking," Jeb protests.

"At night. After you flew your little drone over the area."

Jeb glances at Clem lying on the stone floor of the mine the red and yellow glow of the flare flickers across the wall and Clem's face. His eyes are wide, and bands of sweat are forming across his brow.

"That map you made must be something to see," Joe continues.

Jeb looks at Joe with eyebrows raised.

"Don't be coy, son. We know you're looking for the Shults mine. That little map you have there points to the spot. This spot."

"You got us," Jeb declares. "What can I say? We couldn't resist the appeal of a lost treasure."

"Yeah, you treasure hunters are all the same.

Plenty of fever, but short on brains," Jim scowls.

"Since you found it first, we will be on our way," Jeb smiles. "No harm no foul, right?"

Joe glares at Jeb, and his piercing gaze causes the hair on the back of Jeb's neck to rise. The man behind them moves closer, and Jeb glances at the approaching hulk. Joe stands, pointing his knife at them. "Sorry to say you won't be leaving here," he grumbles. "You found our little piece of heaven."

Clem scrambles to his feet. "You're going to kill us?" he says in a high-pitched squeak.

Joe nods.

"I was forced to come," Clem begs. "He made me," Clem continues, pointing at Jeb as he steps away.

Jeb is slightly irritated at Clem's lack of resolve. He wants to slug the guy, but he *did* bring him here. Jeb casually scans the mineshaft, looking for something he can use against Joe and his accomplice. Aside from the crates of coins, the tunnel is unusually clean. There isn't a shovel or a pick that was left behind.

"Unfortunate for you, son," Joe drawls, "that is the last mistake you will ever make."

"Please don't kill us," Clem begs. "I never saw this place."

Joe ambles closer to them, showing the glinting blade. "Thieves got to pay," Joe says, shrugging his shoulders.

Jeb thinks about grabbing Clem and throwing him at the attackers, but Clem is far too large to throw at anyone. Jeb's heart is pounding against his ribcage as he glances from the large henchman stalking in from back and Joe swinging the knife wildly in front of him.

As the henchman readies to pounce, Jeb steps to the side and grabs his outstretched arm. Jeb performs a perfect Judo throw that sends the larger man flying. With a crash, the man collides with Joe, sending both men to the floor of the tunnel. With the exit blocked, Jeb hops to his feet and grabs Clem by the collar, pulling him deeper into the mineshaft. The red light fades as they race toward the darkness ahead.

Jeb runs as fast as he can, pulling Clem in his wake. He extends his hand, making sure he doesn't run face-first into the wall of the tunnel.

"Get off me!" Joe screams from behind them. "You boys going to pay! You don't know where you're going, but *we* do," he drawls slowly.

"Hurry," Jeb whispers.

The tunnel is damp, and they splash through small puddles, the sound echoing off the narrowing walls of the mine. The air is cool and thick, making it difficult to breath. "How far do you think this goes?" Clem wheezes.

"Legend says it comes out in North Carolina somewhere," Jeb says though gulps of air.

"Oh great," Clem replies.

"Don't worry. I'm working on a plan," Jeb says.

"Who's worried?" Clem bristles. "*I* am! You dragged me on this stupid hunt, and now the

Clampetts are going to kill us!"

Jeb glances behind them. A tiny red dot flickers in the distance. The flare is still burning, but Jeb can't gauge how far they are away from the entrance. They have been slowly navigating the dark tunnel for the last five minutes. He searches for Joe or his hulking accomplice. If they ventured down this far surely they would have a flashlight for the search. Jeb studies the mineshaft silently waiting for a beam of light to dance toward them. No lights. Nothing. Jeb has a bad feeling that Jim and his oversized friend are going to either be hidden in the tunnel ahead of them or be waiting where the mineshaft emerges. There has to be a way out of here that doesn't involve seeing them again.

Jeb stops abruptly in the tunnel, and Clem stops behind him. "Why are we stopping?" Clem says, out of breath.

"We should go back," Jeb says softly.

"What?" Clem protests. "Are you crazy?"

"I think they are going to jump us up ahead," Jeb whispers. "They said they knew where we were going."

"But—"

"I'm going back, and I'm taking the gold with me," Jeb says.

Jeb turns and walks toward the mine entrance with his thumbs looped on the straps of his pack. He isn't worried about bumping into the stone ahead of him because he knows now that the tunnel is straight.

"I shouldn't be doing this," Clem grumbles as he trudges behind Jeb. "You are going to get me killed one of these days," he bristles.

"You enjoy the hunt," Jeb replies.

"I enjoy the *gold*," Clem says.

The red glow from the flare flickers and dies out. A faint white moonglow spills into the tunnel ahead. Jeb can see the outlines of the wooden crates at the base of the stone steps. He turns and places his index finger to his lips. Clem nods, and they stalk quietly toward the stairway. Jeb holds his breath as he steps beside the crate of gold coins. He peers into the frail light, searching for any signs of movement. He can feel the blood pumping in his ears as he strains, listening for Joe or his friend. Jeb would have left someone behind if it were him, and he believes that is what Joe has done.

Satisfied with his survey, Jeb motions toward the box as he places his right hand on the wooden handle. Clem grabs the other side, and slowly and quietly they lift the crate from the stone floor. "*Wow*," Clem grunts as he struggles with the right side. "How much do you think is in here?"

"Enough to make this worth it," Jeb replies, grinning.

Jeb slowly ascends the stone steps. He studies the bent slabs of rock before setting his foot onto the surface. He doesn't want to fall with the hundred or so pounds of gold and silver. That could be a spill he wouldn't make it back from.

As they move closer to the cave entrance, Jeb

surveys the rocks surrounding the opening. Hulk or Joe could be lurking in the shadows as the white light from the moon reflects on the stone surfaces. Jeb spots a shallow dip in the wall, and the shadow moves infinitesimally. "Get ready," Jeb whispers.

"Ready for what?" Clem hisses.

Jeb doesn't answer. His eyes are fixed on the low limestone wall. Instantly, the large man springs from his hiding spot and bounds over the wall. The crate pulls on Jeb's right arm as Clem falls backward. Jeb pulls him forcefully, keeping him from tumbling down the stairs. As Clem regains his balance, the brute rushing toward them swings wildly at Jeb. He ducks the first punch, but the second catches the tip of Jeb's chin. His head jerks backward, and it feels like his head is ready to detach from his body. He releases his grip on the wooden handle, sending the crate crashing into the slab of rock.

Jeb swivels to the right as the attacker swings wildly, narrowly missing his face. Free from the heavy baggage, Jeb moves stealthily around his much larger opponent. "I'm going to enjoy squashing you like a bug," the man jeers as he swivels his neck from side to side. He rushes forward in a whorl, arms swinging menacingly at Jeb's face.

Jeb dodges several strikes and counters with a well-placed jab to the throat.

The man wheezes and staggers in a circle. His nostrils flare, and his eyes are wide with rage. He plows forward without swinging his arms toward Jeb. Jeb tries to shift to the left, but the muscular assailant grabs him and lifts him into the air. Jeb's legs dangle freely, and the air is pressed out of his lungs. It feels like his chest cavity is ready to collapse. The man spits in his face as he squeezes Jeb tighter.

Jeb chops at his neck, but the large muscles deflect his feeble attempts. "You could help," Jeb says weakly, calling to Clem.

"I will take care of you in a minute, boy," the man chortles as he looks at Clem.

Clem is still holding on to the crate handle. His face is white, and he is as rigid as the blocks of stone around him. Jeb's lungs throb in his chest as he tries to take a breath. The laughter of the man is slowed as he swings Jeb from left to right. "Lights out, boy." He laughs.

Jeb's eyes burn, and his brain is slow as he whips through the cool mountain air.

The attacker's face looms large, and his boisterous laugh fills the river valley. "You going to die," he says, laughing boisterously.

Jeb grits his teeth and slams the heel of his palm into the man's nose. With a crunch, the nose is pressed to the man's cheek, and blood is flowing in torrents onto his shirt. Jeb strikes once, then a second time. The man's rib-breaking hug loosens, and Jeb thrusts his palm onto the man's deformed nose. The man howls, and he pulls his hands toward his face, dropping Jeb to the ground.

Jeb takes a few welcome breaths of air and quickly jumps to his feet. He staggers toward the injured assailant. As he nears, he jumps to the top of the rock wall and flies through the air. With a swift kick that collides with the man's face, the attacker falls through the opening to the mineshaft. Jeb lands at the top of the stairs and watches the motionless figure at the bottom.

"I think you k-k-killed him," Clem stammers.

"Better him than us," Jeb replies.

Jeb grabs the handle on the crate of coins and pulls the box—and Clem—behind him. Jeb races around the boulders and the privet and rhododendron along the creek bank. The light glow from the half-moon illuminates the path.

Jeb and Clem trudge through the undergrowth for another two hours. The crate of gold and silver is heavy, but Jeb's spirits are light. The pain in his chin has subsided, and he walks with a wide tooth-bearing smile on his face. He found it. He found the Shults mine. Two years of painstaking research has paid off.

Finally, the forest thins, and they emerge into the clearing where they parked the truck. It is three in the morning, and the lush grass feels soft under their feet. "What are you going to do with your cut of the money?" Jeb asks with a smile.

"Get as far away from you as possible," Clem grunts.

"With this treasure, you should be able to go pretty far." Jeb laughs.

Jeb and Clem carry the crate to the truck, and Jeb opens the door. They slide the wooden box into the back seat with a huff. Jeb slams the door and gets behind the wheel. Clem climbs in the passenger seat and throws his head back. "We made it."

Jeb slaps the steering wheel and laughs. "I told you we would find it," he says. Jeb turns the key, and the truck roars to life. He puts the truck in gear, and as he steps on the gas, Joe jumps in front of the truck with a double-barrel shotgun pointing at the windshield. "You boys going to die!" he yells.

Jeb slams the shifter into reverse and slams his foot on the gas. The truck speeds backward as an explosion erupts from the barrel of the gun. Buckshot sprinkles the hood and windshield, leaving behind tiny divots. Jeb steers away from Joe as he chases them, trying to reload his gun.

The truck hits the dirt road and sprays a cloud of dust. Jeb presses hard on the accelerator, and they leave Joe in a cloud of dust. "Now we can celebrate." Jeb smiles as he looks in the rearview mirror and can see Joe's fading figure in the distance. Another hunt ending in success. Jeb leans his head against the seat and thinks about what he will do next.

CHAPTER 3

Playing on the River

The sun rises over the ridges to the east of Camden, Tennessee, spilling the gold-and-yellow rays of light on the tree-covered landscape. The wide river is calm, with barely a ripple, but the vibrant colors of the sunrise filter across the smooth, reflective surface.

Jeb sits in a white Adirondack chair on the deck of his single-level houseboat: the *Kaiser's Redeemer*. He sips the last drops of his protein shake from a shaker bottle as he watches the calm water in front of him. His paddleboard and open-deck kayak float beside the boat.

The marina is quiet at seven in the morning. Most of the other boats at Brown's Harbor are owned by weekend trippers. Jeb and two retirees are the only permanent residents, and Jeb likes it that way. He likes the serenity of living on the river. It is removed from the hustle and bustle of Camden.

Jeb slips on a pair of water shoes and stands

with a grimace. The fight over the weekend has had its lingering effects. His ribs ache, and the bruises on his face, hands, and side appear to be getting darker. Jeb rubs his jaw as he stands and walks to the edge of the deck. He grabs his paddle and pulls the kayak toward him.

Jeb climbs onto the kayak and sets the paddle on his knees. He pushes away from the boat and drifts backward. His neighbor, Calvin Vincent, emerges from his flat deck boat with a giant cigar in his hand, waving. "Thought I would catch you before you left this morning," Calvin says in a raspy voice. Calvin places his cigar in his mouth and takes a deep draw. Smoke billows from his mouth as he clenches the cigar between his teeth.

"You know my routine," Jeb says with a smile.

"Somebody has to keep an eye on you, son," Calvin says dryly.

"I don't get into too much trouble," Jeb says, shrugging his shoulders.

Jeb has never told Calvin and Sam what he does for a living. He figures it is better they don't know about his professional endeavors.

"Looks like you fell on something," Calvin says, pointing his cigar at the bruises on Jeb's ribs. "You 'don't get into too much trouble." he mimics, eyes narrowing.

"You got me." Jeb laughs.

"It would be safer being a structural engineer," Calvin replies. "I know some guys who could help out with a safe nice-paying job."

"Thanks for the offer," Jeb says, shaking his head, "but I tried it, and it didn't work out."

"If you ever change your mind," Calvin says through a puff of smoke.

"You're next door," Jeb says as he pushes the kayak farther from dock.

Calvin watches Jeb as he drifts backward on the smooth surface of the river. Small ripples fan out from the hull as he cuts through the glassy surface. Jeb pushes the paddle into the water and propels the open kayak toward the open channel. "Oh, I forgot to tell you!" Calvin yells behind him.

Jeb turns his head.

"Someone came by yesterday looking for you. Said they had some business they wanted to discuss!"

Jeb nods and waves as he paddles harder into the current of the river. "Thanks!" Jeb yells as he pushes himself through the resistance of the current, north. Jeb likes the breeze blowing through his hair and across his face as he goes through his routine every morning. He finds peace during his workouts, and they help clear his mind. After another successful venture, Jeb has a thought about taking a few months off. He could catch a flight to Costa Rica and spend a few weeks with friends who own a coffee farm.

Jeb enjoyed his last trip there. Waking up high in the lush green mountains, smelling the tropical flowers. The hikes through the mountains and along the rivers were cathartic to his hectic lifestyle, and it helped that Fran was always there when he was in town.

Fran—a friend from college who also graduated with an engineering degree. Like Jeb, her family had pushed her into going into the family business. Fran, however, had different plans. She joined Sustainable World Farms. The group markets agricultural products around the globe that use natural means of production. Fran likes the travel, and Jeb can't blame her. They both have that kind of free spirit, and they both want a life that doesn't involve sitting in an office, drawing building plans for some firm.

Fran's life had taken her in a direction that didn't involve Jeb.

Seeing Fran again would be fun, he thinks as he paddles along the tree-lined shore. But something he hadn't expected pushes those thoughts out of his mind. Jeb is curious as he strains against the swift-moving current of the river as it moves south, and he pushes his boat north.

"Who came to see me?" he says as he breathes fast. The kayak churns through the rippling water, and Jeb leans forward, pushing the paddle deeper into the pale-green liquid. Jeb's arms ache, and his back throbs as he continues upstream. He pushes past the downtown district, with its Victorian homes positioned on the ridges overlooking the waterway.

Jeb nears Williams Island, a small spit of land in the center of the river. It was a frequent stop for paddleboarders and kayakers who rented the vessels from the downtown outdoor businesses. Williams Island is Jeb's turnaround point on his morning jaunt. He will catch the current south, and the hardest part of his workout will be over. That trip back to the *Kaiser's Redeemer* will give him plenty of time to think about who came to see him. And also, why.

Jeb steers around the tree-filled island and jumps into the flow of the river. He is breathing fast and taking deep gulps of air. The sweat drips off his chin onto the deck of his kayak. He places the paddle on his knees and drifts slowly along the sandy shoreline, watching the city awake. Rush-hour traffic is picking up, filling the roadways with cars.

Jeb smiles as he floats downstream, glad he doesn't have to sit in the gridlock every morning. Every day when he wakes up and goes out on his training exercises, he is one hundred percent sure he made the right choice. He's not an engineer with a corner office and a stable paycheck. He's following his own path, hunting for hidden treasures from the past.

He passes the busy downtown district and returns to the serene, less-stressful parts of Camden. The marina comes into view, and he steers the boat out of the channel, angling toward the slips lining the shore. He paddles toward his slip and ties his kayak to the *Kaiser*. Jeb hops onto the deck and slips his shoes off, throwing them onto the chair.

"Excuse me?"

Jeb turns, and standing on the gangway is a lady with short brown hair that frames her oval face. Her eyes are bright green, and they catch bits of the sun's rays as she looks intently at Jeb.

"Can I help you?" Jeb says as he throws his paddle onto the deck. He grabs a towel hanging on the chair and wipes the sweat from his face and hair.

The woman steps up to the railing and places her hands on the worn metal. Jeb notices her fingers are long, pale, and delicate like a piano player. "You are Jeb Strauss?" she asks sternly.

Jeb ruffles his hair with the towel, and after he finishes, he throws the towel onto the back of the chair. "Who wants to know?" Jeb says, studying her pale face.

"I need help finding something," she says sadly.

"And you think this Jeb Strauss guy can help?" Jeb replies.

"I heard he is the best."

Not many people know that Jeb is a treasure hunter. There are maybe four or five people that know his real occupation. He is more interested in who told this woman about his life than in her wanting to find something. "Who would say a thing like that?" Jeb laughs as he sits in his Adirondack chair and places his feet on a small table.

"Are you Jeb Strauss or not?" she says bluntly. Her cheeks redden as she places her hands on her hips.

Jeb links his fingers behind his head and rocks slowly backward. "No need to get angry," he says with a smile. "I'm Jeb, but I don't find things. I'm an engineer."

Her face softens, and she points to the deck. "May I come aboard?"

Jeb motions toward the other chair. She steps gently from the gangplank onto the moving boat deck. She moves swiftly to the chair and repositions it so it faces Jeb. She doesn't sit but stands, her hands gripping the back of the chair.

"Let's not waste each other's time, Mr. Strauss," she starts.

Jeb drops his feet from the table and leans forward, rubbing his chin with his right hand. He is intrigued by her directness. "Fair enough." He motions for her to sit, and she walks around the chair and sits, facing him. A small smile forms as she crosses her legs.

CHAPTER 4

The Story

The woman sits with her back straight, her deep-green eyes set on Jeb. He watches her, curiously trying to get a read on her. Though he is only twenty-four, Jeb is adept at figuring out a person's motives and intentions. This lady, though, is little more formidable. She seems shrewd and calculating. She hasn't revealed too much yet, and that could pose a problem.

She places her hands on her knee. "Mr. Strauss."

Jeb shakes his head. "Jeb," he says, smiling. "I'm not my old man."

The woman clears her throat. "Mr. Strauss, I am Margaret Armstrong," she says formally. "There is something that is very important to my family that I would like you to help me locate," Margaret says in a strong voice.

Jeb has never been asked to find something for someone before. His method of operation is finding a local legend pertaining to lost gold or silver. After researching, if it is probable there is something to the story, he will spend the money for an expedition. Most legends don't make it through the research phase.

He scratches his chin and looks toward the water. "We talking gold, silver, or something else?"

Margaret is silent for a minute, and Jeb looks at her blank face. Her green eyes sparkle as she taps her finger on her knee. "There are gold coins on the ship that sank, but I have no interest in the riches. What I am after is something that belonged to my great-great-grandfather."

Jeb leans forward, elbows on his knees, stroking his chin with his right hand. *This could be an interesting story to get involved in*, he thinks as he searches her face. There is no emotion in her features. The only response she gives is the drumming of her fingers on her knee.

"Not after the gold?" Jeb says sarcastically.

"That is correct," Margaret replies.

"What is it? A family heirloom?"

"You could say that," Margaret responds coldly.

"Suppose I agree to your offer. What do I get out of it?" Jeb says.

"You get all the gold," Margaret says.

Jeb rubs his hands together, thinking quickly about the offer. He gets all the treasure. He studies her, but she remains stone-faced. She blinks as blandly as she speaks. "How much we talking about?" Jeb asks, eyes narrowed.

She stares at Jeb with her intense, calculating eyes. "Thirty million," she says, uninterested.

Jeb whistles as he leans into his chair. This one would be far better than the mine take, and it could be less dangerous. Though Margaret is secretive, surely finding some old family treasure would be less hazardous than the goons he encountered in the mountains over the weekend. "I'm going to need background information so I can get started," Jeb says calmly.

Margaret nods. "Of course."

"Can I get you a drink or something before you start?" Jeb says as he stands.

"No thank you," Margaret replies.

Jeb opens the door to the houseboat. "I'll be right back," he says as he enters the dark living room. The only furniture in the room is a red leather sofa and a high-back sitting chair positioned around an oval wooden table. The room is orderly and neat. Jeb stops at the table and grabs a thick brown notebook. He pulls a black pen from the spine and walks toward the door.

Margaret is still sitting with her hands on her knee as Jeb emerges from the interior. He smiles and sits, opening his notebook. "When you are ready," Jeb says as he touches the tip of his pen to his tongue. Margaret takes a deep breath.

"The story begins with my great-great-grandfather John Armstrong. He was the captain of a steamship that operated along the Tennessee

River during the Civil War. The *Baron* transported food and supplies from Bridgeport to the besieged Union forces in Chattanooga. On one of his trips, he transported a crate that General Grant requisitioned personally. It was not on the manifest, and the men transporting the package were very secretive about its contents. My great-great-grandfather, being the reliable captain he was, didn't ask questions. He delivered the package to Chattanooga and returned to Bridgeport."

Jeb new a little about the history of the Battle of Chattanooga. How the Confederates wanted to starve the Union soldiers and force them out of the vital city. Grant had decided the city was important to the future plans of the western theater, so he placed General Thomas in command and told him to hold the city. The Unionist won the three-day battle in the end, forcing the Confederates farther south.

That is the extent of his knowledge. Jeb is intrigued by the story: undocumented crates of unknown materials requested by U. S. Grant to be delivered to the general in Chattanooga. What could be in those crates? Maybe that is the gold Margaret mentioned earlier.

"After a few days, there was another crate and then another. For a week, the deliveries were consistent. Then, on November 10, Captain Armstrong was given a shipment that contained four crates, and the accompanying troops guarding the shipment were unlike the normal officers. They didn't speak, and they always had their pistols drawn. My great-great-grandfather thought this was odd, but it was his duty to deliver the package to the besieged men in Chattanooga. Unfortunately, on the way from Bridgeport, the vessel was lost, along with Captain Armstrong."

Margaret's voice trails away as she looks toward the water. Jeb can sense that, for the first time since she came aboard, there is a hint of feeling in her words. Whatever she is looking for must be extremely important.

A sunken steamer from the Civil War could be difficult to find. The vessel has been underwater for 150 years. Jeb's mind works quickly, thinking through the course of action he will take.

"The story doesn't end there," Margaret says is a soft voice. "The US Army never went looking for the ship. The *Baron* was never recovered, and the interesting part is, it was erased from all reports and correspondence. It was like the *Baron* and Captain Armstrong never existed."

Margaret stands, arms at her sides, and back as straight as a board. "I hope the story alone is enough to pique your interest and help me find Captain Armstrong."

Jeb looks at her as he strokes his chin. He stands, smiling. "I think I can find the ship," he says confidently. "I will get to work as quickly as possible."

"Thank you," she replies. "Discretion is important. No one can know what you are looking for or who has paid you."

"Of course," Jeb smiles. "You won't have any trouble there."

"I will be in touch," she says, and she walks toward the gangplank. She steps from the boat deck effortlessly and swiftly leaves the marina. Jeb watches her walk all the way to the parking lot, where her black Cadillac CTS is parked.

"What you got yourself into now, son?" Calvin says from the deck of his boat.

Jeb doesn't look at him. His focus is on the Cadillac leaving the marina parking area.

"That lady gives off some bad vibes," Calvin continues.

Jeb shakes his head. "Maybe, but her job should be a lot of fun," Jeb says with a smile.

CHAPTER 5

The Diary

Jeb thought about taking a few days to relax, but the curiosity of Margaret's story got the better of him. He showered quickly, and he now sits at the table in the galley, searching on his laptop. The hours have ticked by, and it is now one in the afternoon. Page after page of searches, and nothing that mentions Captain Armstrong or the Baron. If the US government doesn't recognize the ship as having existed, then there is a high probability that any evidence available won't be on any searchable database. History is a funny area of study. The victor writes the narrative, and if they didn't want to find the Baron, it would not be found.

Jeb closes the laptop and pinches the bridge of his nose. No official records. How do you go about finding something that doesn't exist? *What do you know?* Jeb stares at the ceiling. "I know that the vessel was lost somewhere between Bridgeport, Alabama, and Chattanooga, Tennessee," Jeb says, rubbing his face. "That leaves about fifty miles of river to explore," he continues, shaking his head.

That is too much area for lucking into finding the ship. Jeb stands and grabs his keys. He needs to get information, and that is going to require a visit to Montlake College. Dr. Russell Wright is someone he has used many times when he has come to a dead end. Dr. Wright is an expert in colonial and Civil War history.

Jeb steps into the afternoon heat of Camden. Eighty-five degrees with sixty percent humidity makes it feel like he's breathing through a moist cloth. He hops onto the gangway and strides toward the marina parking area. Jeb pulls a pair of Ray-Ban sunglasses over his eyes as he walks from the covered awning to his car. He unlocks the black Saab and opens the door slowly. He scans the area around his car, looking for anything that might be out of the ordinary.

Jeb is always cautious, and after the weekend he had, it might be prudent to be even more careful. Satisfied, he settles into the seat and turns the key. The engine comes to life, and he closes the door. He shoves the gearshift forward and speeds away from the marina, kicking dust and smoke into the air behind him.

He drives like a professional through the narrow, curvy streets of Camden. He speeds around cars in the slow and fast lanes as he weaves through the afternoon traffic. He turns right with a squeal of the tires onto Vine Street. The tree-lined avenue is filled with two-story Victorian homes with large white columns and second-floor decks. Many of the professors from the college live in this part of campus. He races by a sign that reads "35," and instantly he looks into the rearview mirror, searching for the campus police.

No police behind him, but a silver Crown Victoria is keeping pace with him. He presses the gas and races ahead, sailing through the residential district. Jeb checks the speedometer. Sixty. He glances in the mirror, and the Crown Vic is still there. Jeb downshifts and rips the steering wheel to the left. As he turns onto Oak Street, puffs of white smoke drift from the tires. He presses the gas and speeds along the straight roadway.

Jeb looks into the mirror, and the silver car makes the turn onto Oak Street. "Somebody has an interest in me," Jeb says as he slows to the posted speed limit. The car behind him slows, as well. "I guess he wants me to know he's there," Jeb continues. Jeb drives the rest of the way, watching the car behind him.

Jeb turns his car into the parking lot of a three-story brick building. Holt Hall is in tall, white block letters on a sign in front of the building. Jeb watches his mirror as the silver sedan slows and drives by the building. It continues down the street until it is out of view. Jeb turns the car off and studies the area outside the car.

He has second thoughts about visiting Dr. Wright today. What if the Crown Vic comes back? What if there are more of them? "No need to worry.," Jeb says, chuckling. "I can handle them." There are a few students with backpacks walking on the sidewalk beside the building. April is the end of the semester for the students, and it appears that most of the undergraduates have gone home.

Jeb climbs out of his car and scans the bushes beside the entrance. He looks at the windows of Holt Hall and the windows of the adjacent buildings. Satisfied that all is normal, he grabs a small bag from the console and shoves it in his pocket. He closes the door and looks around one more time. He chuckles again as he walks toward the glass door. He takes the steps two at a time and hurries into the lobby of the building.

*****

Jeb taps on the office door of Dr. Wright. "Come in," says a deep, thundering voice from inside. Jeb turns the knob and walks into a well-lit room. The walls are lined with awards and covers of books written by Dr. Wright. The large bookcase behind the polished wooden desk is filled with books.

Dr. Wright is a short man with a thick gray

mustache and a pointed goatee. He looks at Jeb as he enters, pointing toward a chair in front of the desk. "Hope you don't mind me dropping by unannounced.," Jeb says as he sits.

"Always a pleasure to see you." Dr. Wright says.

"I have a few questions about some local history." Jeb replies.

"Before we get to your current query, how did the last endeavor work out?" Dr. Wright asks, pulling on his goatee.

A smile stretches across Jeb's face.

"Your reaction tells the story," Dr. Wright says, slapping the table. "So, the mine still exists?"

Jeb nods. "A few complications, but yes, the mine is there," Jeb says, laughing. Jeb throws a small brown sack the size of small marble bag onto the desk.

Dr. Wright looks at the canvas material and slowly grabs the bag. He shakes it lightly, and a clinking sound emerges from the enclosed contents. "It's heavy," Dr. Wright chuckles as he opens a drawer and drops the sack inside.

"Those survey documents helped," Jeb replies.

"Good. Good," Dr. Wright says enthusiastically. "You have something new, yes?"

"Just a few preliminary questions. I'm not sure if this thing even exists."

Dr. Wright leans back in his chair, green eyes bright and wide.

"I heard a story about a steamer called the *Baron*."

Jeb watches Dr. Wright's face to see if the name registers. Dr. Wright's eyes narrow, and he runs his fingers through his goatee.

"You ever heard of it?" Jeb asks.

Dr. Wright looks vacantly across the desk. He slowly shakes his head. "Can't say that I have," Dr. Wright replies.

That isn't what Jeb wanted to hear. He had hoped that a steamer carrying gold would be something Dr. Wright would have heard about.

"It was a steamer that shuttled troops from Bridgeport, Alabama, to Chattanooga, Tennessee, during the siege in 1863," Jeb says.

The professor pulls on the tip of his goatee. "Never heard of it. You sure it was operating on the Tennessee?" Dr. Wright exhales.

"Yep. It made the Chattanooga run for a few weeks At least that is what my client believes.," Jeb responds.

"Did it have another name?" Dr. Wright questions.

"I am not sure about that. Like I said. My client believes that this vessel operated on the river at that time.," Jeb says dejectedly.

"Maybe the story is bad," Dr. Wright says with a grimace.

"It's possible," Jeb says, smiling. He places his hands on the desk and stands. "Thank you for your time, Dr. Wright."

Dr. Wright nods. "Anytime. Sorry I couldn't be of more help."

Jeb shakes Dr. Wright's hand. "Don't spend it all in one place." Jeb says, smiling. Jeb walks toward the door and grabs the handle. He turns. "One more thing. Have you ever heard of Captain John Armstrong? My client says this was the captain of the ship."

Dr. Wright shakes his head. "Never."

Jeb opens the door. "Thanks." he says as he walks out of the room, closing the door behind him.

*****

Jeb exits Holt Hall and walks along the tree-lined sidewalk. He is lost in thought as he moves toward his Saab. A treasure hunt without any information isn't a hunt at all. The research is the most important part to finding anything that is hidden. If the government wiped the *Baron* from military records, how is he going to find it? In their view, the ship and Captain Armstrong never existed.

He opens the door, and sitting on his front seat is an old, tattered brown book with the golden initials "F. D." printed on the front cover. Jeb cautiously grabs the book and turns it over. The leather binding is frayed, and the pages between the cover are yellow. He looks from the book to the surrounding area. The street is empty, and there are only a few students walking along the sidewalk. He doubts any of them left the book in his car.

Jeb throws the book on the passenger seat and climbs inside. He looks through the windshield toward Holt Hall. Nobody watching him from in there, either. Jeb starts the car and puts it in reverse. He slowly backs the car into the traffic lane. He spots the silver Crown Vic at the end of the street. Jeb's pulse quickens, and he flexes his fingers on the steering wheel. He shoves the car into first gear and spins the tires as he presses the gas too hard. The rear of the car turns as he pulls onto the main road. "Did you leave me something?" Jeb asks as he shifts quickly through the gears. The engine revs as he presses the gas.

The silver car races off down Walnut Street at a high rate of speed. Jeb can't see the person driving, but he is going to catch them. Jeb steers his Saab wildly onto Walnut, swerving as he reacts to a mail truck driving in the opposite direction. The Crown Victoria turns right at the next intersection ahead. Jeb presses his foot to the floor and accelerates to sixty miles per hour. The intersection comes upon him quickly, and his tires screech as he hits the brakes to make the turn.

Cars swerve out of his path as he speeds along Cherry Street. The silver car is nowhere in sight. Jeb slams his hand against the steering wheel as he drives farther north along the four-lane road. He slows the car and searches the cross streets he passes. Nothing there, either. Jeb glances at the book in the passenger seat. "Time to see what is inside," he says as he drives along the busy street.

CHAPTER 6

The Baron

The sun sets over the ridges around Camden, showering the hills and valleys with orange-and-yellow light. Jeb sits on the deck of his houseboat with the tattered book in his hand. He twirls a pencil between his fingers as he reads the faded writing on the brittle yellow pages. "F. D." are the initials of a man named Friedrich Delashmitt. He was a deckhand on a steam ship called the USS Chattanooga, and the diary is an account of his work along the Tennessee River in 1863. He was there on the day of the launch.

October 24, 1863. We set the tub to the water, and she took to it like a Canada goose. A slight rock from port to starboard, but I believe we can transport the rations and munitions to our boys.

October 26, 1863. We finished stabilizing and fitting the decking for cargo. The quartermaster said that time was of the essence, and work on the vessel continues in earnest. Our mission is ready to commence any day. I do feel for the men we have been charged with rescuing. I can only imagine their desperation as they starve.

Jeb writes the dates and descriptions in his own notebook. He also traces a small map F. D. had drawn of the river in his notebook. The small black line winds between ridges as he traverses southeastern Tennessee along the page.

October 29, 1863. We are set with two barges affixed, loaded with salted pork and hard tack. We have a forty-five-mile journey ahead of us. I hope we do not meet any Rebels. A musket ball can make it across the river. There is no place for us to hide if we meet them.

Jeb stares at his notes. There is no mention of the *Baron*. From what the journal says, there was only one steamer operating on the river in November of 1863. He pinches the bridge of his nose.

The last rays of sunlight glitter on the smooth surface as the sun slowly sets behind the ridge. Jeb rubs his eyes and yawns loudly. "Going to need more coffee," Jeb sighs as he throws the journal on the table and walks into his houseboat. He hurriedly brews a steaming cup of black coffee and walks back to his table on the deck.

The lights along the gangplank of the marina illuminate the *Kaiser* and the other boats rocking slowly on the ripples of the water. The hills and forests around the marina are shrouded in darkness. Jeb falls into the seat and takes a sip from the steaming mug. He takes the diary from the table and carefully turns the pages. "Where are you?" he asks as his eyes dart from one side of the page to the other.

November 7, 1863. It is the darkest night we have experienced since we began ferrying supplies. The only lights are the campfires on the bank. We aren't sure if they are from our troops or the Rebels. The captain instructed us to stay alert and to push to the other side of the river. It is so dark we can't see the water. We can hear it sloshing along the hull of the steamer. With all the turns in this channel, I'm certain we could run aground. Out of the darkness, we heard a rumble and what sounded like a smaller vessel cutting through the water. A voice yelled in the night, "Make way! Make way!" The captain quickly gave the order to correct course. Later, I found out there is another steamer working along the river. We have never seen the ship or the crew at Bridgeport, but some of our men say they are transporting bullion from the front. Not sure if I believe it, but this phantom I heard tonight is working our course along the river. Philip says he saw the captain once. He said his name is Armstrong, but again, I have never seen or heard of anyone by that name.

Jeb grabs his pencil and feverishly scribbles across the page in his notebook. His pulse quickens. He needs to cross-reference this account to make sure F. D. was a real person stationed in Bridgeport in 1863. Jeb finishes writing and quickly grabs his laptop. He types feverishly, checking the military records for Friedrich Delashmitt. In a few seconds, the articles appear on the screen. "Friedrich Delashmitt, US Army. 1862–1865, Army of the Tennessee." Jeb smiles broadly as he stares absently at the screen.

He hasn't found the "X" on the map yet, but there is some corroboration to the story. Jeb closes the screen on the computer and places it in his bag. He grabs F.D.'s journal from the table and places it in the pocket of the bag. He will look over the rest of it in the morning. Jeb checks his watch. It is eleven-thirty. Jeb yawns loudly and slowly grabs his bag from the floor. He throws the bag over his shoulder and walks to the door. He glances toward the parking lot, and a dark sedan is parked near the road.

Jeb knows all the cars at the marina, and this one doesn't belong to anyone who lives here. He holds the strap of his bag tightly in his hands as he looks at the car. He hopes there is someone inside, rather than them skulking around where he can't see them. His eyes dart from the sedan to the gangway. The marina is silent except for the light splashing off water against the hull of the boats.

Jeb steps cautiously toward the edge of his houseboat and peers along the sides. He looks from the water level to the top. Satisfied with his search, he carefully opens the door and peers inside. There is nowhere to hide in the living room. The couch, chair, and table are the only furniture. There is no one in the kitchen, either.

He looks toward the sedan, and a silhouette of a head moves. Jeb grips the bag tighter. Someone is in the car. Are there others around? Cold sweat drips onto his nose from his brow. This is a time he wishes he carried his .38 all the time. The revolver is safely inside his desk in the bedroom—the last place he needs to search.

He takes a last look at the black car and, satisfied the occupant is still there, slowly closes the door behind him. His footfalls are silenced by the shag carpeting. He walks through the living room and quietly through the kitchen. His bedroom door is closed, and he quietly nears it. He stops and places his ear as close to the paneled door as he can. He listens, holding his breath, straining to hear anything from inside.

The boat rocks slightly, causing Jeb to shift his weight to his right leg. More sweat drips from his brow onto his nose and chin. He grasps the door handle firmly. Jeb's hands are sweaty and cold as he touches the cold metal. "Time to see what's behind door number two," he mumbles to himself.

Jeb throws the door open and barrels inside, swinging his bag wildly in front of him. His eyes dart from his perfectly made bed to the writing desk along the wall. Empty. He checks under the bed and in the bathroom, but all the places where someone could be hiding are empty. Jeb walks quickly to his desk and open the drawer. His .38 revolver is missing. The sweat dripping from his face is cold. He opens the other drawers, but they are empty.

"You should always be prepared," says a man in a dark suit and thick glasses. Jeb turns quickly and the man is standing in the doorway of his bedroom. The man has a thin mouth with thin lips pressed together. He is pointing the barrel of the revolver at Jeb's chest.

"Hey, wait a minute," Jeb says with one hand open, palm up toward the stranger, and the other holding his bag. "I don't know what you want."

The man looks at Jeb blankly without blinking. "You are looking for something that is not meant to be found," the man in black finally says without emotion. "There is no Captain Armstrong. There is no *Baron*," he continues.

Jeb is cold as he glares at the intruder. He could throw his bag at the guy, but studying the man and his demeanor, Jeb is certain he would be dead before his bag found its mark. "What do you want?" Jeb asks.

"Stop searching," the man responds coldly. "This will be your only warning."

The light in the bedroom flickers and is extinguished. Jeb falls behind the bed and peers over the mattress. The room is quiet and still. He waits, holding his breath, straining to hear any movement from the man. After five excruciating minutes, Jeb decides the threat has passed. He climbs from behind the bed and cautiously walks toward the door. Jeb looks into the living room, and it is empty. He hurries to the front door and peers outside. The dark sedan is gone. He turns, and his pistol is sitting on the table with one bullet pointed toward the ceiling.

Jeb grabs the revolver and places it in his pocket. He snatches the bullet from the table and examines the gold casing. It isn't one of his. On the side of the casing, etched in the gold, there is a shield with a triangle on top. "Interesting." Jeb says as he places the round into his pocket. "Something else to figure out I guess," he says as he stares out the window.

CHAPTER 7

Missing Pieces

Jeb woke up early and paddled an extra mile up the river. He needed to get his thoughts together so he could plan his day. He made it back to his boat at seven-thirty. The air is thick and listless. Jeb steps out onto the deck, his hair wet from the shower and canvas bag thrown over his shoulder.

Jeb checks the parking area for any unwelcome visitors and, satisfied that everything is normal, he climbs onto the gangway.

"Where you going today?" Calvin asks as he sprays his boat with water.

"Going to work," Jeb says, smiling.

"This life is going to get you in a world of trouble, Jeb," Calvin says sternly.

Jeb thinks about the man who visited his house last night. Problems are currently increasing at an alarming rate. "What's life without a little adventure?" Jeb says, shrugging as he walks toward the parking lot.

"Be careful out there, son!" Calvin yells. "Been some visitors around that don't belong here."

Jeb waves without turning and walks with determination.

Jeb opens the door of his Saab. He looks around the lot, but all the cars are ones he recognizes. Jeb surveys the street, but this area of Camden is quiet this time of the morning. He places his bag in the passenger seat. The journal, his notebook, and his revolver are safely inside. Jeb thinks it is a good idea to always keep his pistol on him. He wants to be prepared for a chance meeting with the man who visited him last night. Jeb has a feeling they are watching him very closely.

*****

Jeb drives along Old Highway 41 through southeast Tennessee. The route was once filled with motels and eateries, but that was in the distant past. He passes an old boarded-up gas station as he drives between the vibrant-green ridges that extend from the edge of the road. An old red pickup truck passes him, and the old driver extends his hand in a friendly wave. Jeb likes the drive—it is much more relaxed than the interstate.

He presses the gas as the road turns to the right at the base of a ridge. The Tennessee River comes into view, and Jeb glances at the slow-moving water. He wants to see the route of the river and get a feel for the landscape. A crane flies overhead as the roadway straightens, and he accelerates.

Jeb watches the rearview mirror, but he hasn't spotted a tail yet. Another fifteen minutes, he drives across the bridge in Haletown. This is the spot along the river he wants to explore. Bridgeport is south of this point, and Jeb figures he can find the path of the *Baron* from the descriptions in the journal. Investigating the river could give him some clues about possible resting places for the wreck.

He stops at the Spine Ridge Hiking Trail Center. It is a small brick building with a lobby and bathrooms. He parks his Saab facing the road, and he watches the highway for a few minutes before exiting the car. He grabs his bag and takes his notebook from the interior. He walks along the gravel trail that loops around a pine-and-oak thicket. The birds chirp loudly from the trees as he walks by. The beauty of the outdoors is one of the perks of his current line of work. If he were engineering, he would be stuck in an office with self-absorbed, miserable people.

His internship at Consolidated Partners his final year of college cemented his current career for him. Jeb had hated every morning he had to go into the office. The engineers in the office were a miserly group of pretentious, arrogant, elitists he could not work with. He was happy when the semester finally ended and he was able to leave the engineering field and its personalities behind. Besides, treasure hunting paid well, and it offered plenty of adventure.

Jeb emerges from the trees and steps out into the bright sunlight. The rays reflect brightly off the brownish-green surface of the slow-moving river. Water splashes on the rocks at the bank as a great white cabin-cruiser plows through the water. The roar of the engine sends the birds fluttering and flying in all directions. He watches the boat, hands shielding his eyes from the bright reflection.

On the top deck of the cruiser is a man with a pair of binoculars, searching the shoreline. Jeb isn't sure if he is just an avid bird-watcher, but he bets they are looking for him. The man turns the binoculars and stops when he sees Jeb. Jeb smiles and waves his hand tauntingly at the mysterious figure on the boat. The man keeps his glasses fixed on Jeb, and the boat slows, making a long, arching turn.

Jeb lowers his hand quickly and places his hand in his bag. His fingers wrap around the grip of his revolver, and he presses the safety, engaging the weapon. He thinks of running, but something tells him that since they didn't blast away from their position, they might be willing to talk.

The large white vessel slows as it nears Jeb standing along the bank. The engine slows, and the boat drifts on the current about ten yards off shore. A man wearing a crisp white shirt and dark sunglasses stands at the railing. "Maggie said you would be down at some point and to keep an eye out for you," he says with a thick Southern drawl.

Jeb didn't know anyone named Maggie. Maybe the man has him mixed up with someone else. "Excuse me?" Jeb says.

"Oh shoot, *Margaret*," he says, shaking his head. "She told me a guy that looks a lot like you would be down, needing a tour of the river."

Jeb relaxes his grip on the gun. "Margaret sent you? How did she know I would be coming?" Jeb asks, eyes narrowed.

"I keep the boat over at that marina," the man says, pointing toward the other side of the river. "And she told me to be looking for a guy with glasses and short hair driving a Saab. There aren't many of those left on the road, you know. So, I said I would," he says, laughing. "My name is Scotty. Scotty Ford. You ready for your tour?"

Jeb looks north and south along the river. There aren't any other boats along this stretch of the river. Jeb is uneasy about jumping on a boat after the meeting he had the previous night. "I think I will get my own boat for the tour."

Scotty laughs loudly, and his guffaws echo across the water. He holds his hands up. "I'm here to help you, brother," Scotty says. "You can come aboard and check things out if you like."

Jeb grasps his revolver. "What does Margaret

look like?" Jeb asks, studying Scotty's face.

"I see what you're doing. Good technique. Can't be too careful," Scotty says with a nod. "Short brown hair, eyes like emeralds, and pale as smoke on the water."

The description is perfect, and Jeb feels a bit more at ease with that information.

"Come on, boy!" Scotty bellows. "We're burning daylight here."

Jeb looks from where he is on the bank to where the boat in rocking on the current. He didn't intend on getting wet today, but it's for the treasure. He slings his bag over his shoulder and steps into the water. He walks through the soft silt and clay on the river bottom. Finally, he reaches the boat, and Scotty is there, arm extended. "Get on up here," Scotty says.

Jeb grasps Scotty's hand. He pulls him onto the deck of the cruiser. Scotty hands him a towel. "Let's get going," Scotty says as he stands behind the controls.

Jeb takes his field book from his pack and stands at the railing. The engine roars as Scotty pushes the throttle forward. The boat lurches forward, sending water spraying onto the deck. Jeb wipes the water droplets from his book as they race upstream through the tree-covered ridges.

The wind whips the flags violently as Scotty slows the cruiser to idling speed. They are in a narrow portion of the Tennessee River that bends to the east and then to the west. The foot of each ridge extends to the river's edge, casting dark shadows across the surface. Jeb takes his pencil from his book and traces the lines he has drawn there. The map of the waterway from F. D.'s journal does not match what Jeb is seeing. The river has changed since 1863, and Jeb had thought that might happen, since TVA had flooded large portions of the valley when they built dams along the river. This is going to make the search for Armstrong's ship much harder.

Jeb walks toward the helm and stands beside Scotty. He holds his book so the captain can see the drawing. "You think this curved line corresponds to that ridge extending toward the river?" Jeb asks, pointing toward the distant mountain.

"This is the gorge, boy. All the ridges look the same," Scotty replies, smiling.

Scotty is right. Each of the angular structures extends toward the river, and each one terminates at the water's edge. Jeb surveys his notebook and finds a point where a large tributary merges with the Tennessee. "Does this stream still flow into the river?" Jeb asks.

Scotty looks at the drawing with curiosity, like it is the first map of a waterway he has ever seen. "The only tributary that large near the gorge is Suck Creek," Scotty replies.

That name is mentioned in the journal. Jeb rifles through his bag and pulls the worn, leatherbound book from its depths. He has yellow pieces of paper placed in the book, with numbers written on them. He turns to the tab with the number ten on it.

November 8, 1863 The passage through the gorge is treacherous and deadly. Even the most experienced river pilot gets nervous when navigating the narrows. But the deadliest place on our journey to and from Chattanooga is the Suck. The Suck is a powerful whirlpool created by the torrent of water flowing from a steep mountain stream into the river. We have been lucky thus far, but we have heard tales of boats being pulled into the whirlpool.

On the piece of yellow paper, Jeb has drawn a map of the river with Suck Creek flowing into the main channel. He draws a large circle on the map. "Take me there." he says.

Scotty salutes. "You're the boss." He starts the engine with a roar, and he pushes the throttle forward. The boat cuts through the water with ease as they turn along the meandering channel through the encroaching ridges.

Jeb keeps his eyes on the river, carefully scanning the surface and the bank. He scribbles hurriedly in his book, adding very specific descriptions of the terrain and the time between each marker. The wind roars in his ears as they cut through the choppy greenish-brown water. A bald eagle flies over the boat, inspecting this large interloper of the serene river gorge. Jeb places his pencil behind his ear carefully placing the old journal into his bag. He stands and shoves his book into his pocket. He walks cautiously toward the railing of the boat, looking toward the shore.

Jeb hears a *thud* after something strikes the wooden railing of the boat. Another *thud* in the exact same place. "Somebody is shooting at us!" Jeb yells as he stumbles over to the wheel. Jeb's heart is beating wildly in his chest as he hides behind the thin metal sheeting of the cabin.

"What did you say?" Scotty yells over the roaring engine.

Thud. Thud. Thud. Three bullets tear through the cabin and strike against the wooden decking, narrowly missing Scotty and Jeb. "They're shooting at us!" Scotty yells.

"Get us out of here!" Jeb screams, peering through the holes in the sheet metal.

"You don't have to tell me." Scotty grumbles. He pushes the throttle ahead full. The engine screams as jets of water spew from the stern.

Jeb holds on to the deck rail as they careen to the right.

Ping. Ping. More bullets hit the cabin and the side of the cruiser. "They're destroying my boat!" Scotty yells.

"It's going to be *us* if you don't get us through this pass!" Jeb screams.

Jeb has never been this scared in his life. It is like being in a war zone as the bullets strike continually around him. That is automatic fire coming from somewhere along the shore, and there is more than one shooter. Jeb ducks and shuffles toward the rear of the cabin. He rifles through his bag, pulling out his pistol. It won't do much against a target a hundred yards away, but it does make him feel better.

He scans the shoreline as Scotty steers the boat toward the eastern shore. A bullet strikes the floor, sending a puff of dust into Jeb's eyes. He wipes the particulates away quickly with his shaking right hand. "That was a little too close." Jeb growls as he hides behind the wall. He searches the tree line along the curved river, but there isn't a sign of the shooters.

Suddenly, a revving speed boat dashes by the cabin cruiser, spraying their boat with a new hail of bullets. The bullets tear through the thin metal of the cabin, sending metallic shards falling to the wooden deck. Jeb crawls along the deck, pointing his revolver at the white-and-red boat pacing their movement upstream. Jeb's ears are ringing as he fires a shot at the waterline of the pursuing craft. His bullet penetrates the hull above the waterline. As he lines up a second shot, a blast of rifle fire explodes in the air above him. A shower of splintered wood and torn metal rain down on him.

The cabin cruiser sputters, and smoke billows from the engine. A few rounds must have struck the motor. The boat veers toward the eastern shore in a jerky manner. Sweat pours from Jeb's brow as he looks toward the helm. Captain Scotty is slumped over the controls, and a dark-red pool forms around his feet. "Scotty?" Jeb whispers as he crawls toward the captain.

Jeb takes cover behind the helm beside the

pooling blood. He looks over the wheel, but he can't see their attackers. He instinctively grabs Scotty and lowers his body to the floor. Blood flows continually from a small hole in his shoulder. Another hole has torn the muscle loose in his forearm. Jeb breathes a sigh of relief. Scotty is alive, and Jeb tears the end of his own shirt and ties the strip of cloth around Scotty's bicep. The blood stops flowing from the wound on his forearm, but the hole in his shoulder continues pouring.

Jeb tears another strip of fabric from his shirt and forms it into a ball. He shoves the rolled bit of cloth into the deep red tear in Scotty's shoulder. Scotty screams, and his eyes spring open. His pupils are dilated, and his eyes dart from Jeb to the destruction of the cabin. "They tore up my boat pretty good." Scotty says, gritting his teeth.

"Tore you up pretty good, too." Jeb replies as he presses Scotty's shoulder.

"I couldn't tell how many there were." Scotty growls.

"Maybe two boats with some guys on the shore." Jeb replies.

The boat rolls to the right as something hits the port side. Scotty slides a few inches in the thick red liquid on the wooden deck. "You're going to get us out of here." Scotty spits.

Jeb nods as he continues applying pressure.

"It's fine." Scotty growls.

Jeb removes his bloody hands from Scotty's shoulder and peers through the splintered wheel.

Jeb carefully grasps the throttle and pushes it all the way forward.

The engine whines and sputters, and puffs of smoke rise from the damaged boat. Finally, the engine roars to life. Jeb grasp the remnants of the helm and steers toward the western bank. Ahead, Jeb sees the red-and-white boat speeding toward them. He can see a tall man with long dark-brown hair and sunglasses steering and a man with a military-style haircut and chiseled face pointing a semiautomatic rifle toward him.

Bullets hit the deck in front of the helm, sending dust and wood fragments flying into the air. Jeb pulls the wheel to port and presses the throttle forward. *Thunk. Thunk. Thunk.* Bullets rip through the hull as Jeb makes the turn and races away from his pursuers. The water sprays behind the boat as more shots sink into the wooden planking. Jeb doesn't dare look backward. Sweat pours across his face, and his heart races. Being shot at is relatively new to Jeb, and he doesn't care for it.

"How you doing, Scotty?" Jeb says, wiping the sweat from his brow.

"As good as ever." Scotty wheezes. The deck is slick from the blood. Scotty is slumped against the helm at Jeb's feet.

"We will be back to the bridge in a few minutes." Jeb says, "I don't think these guys want to draw attention to themselves."

"Probably not." Scotty utters softly.

Pushing the cabin cruiser as fast as it will

go, Jeb hopes they will make it out of the confined and deserted river course of the gorge. Jeb sees the last confining promontory one hundred yards ahead. After that, they will be at their starting point. There are plenty of people at the trailhead. Suddenly, Jeb catches sight of a green-and-white blur in his peripheral vision. Before he can brace himself, the boat jerks upward, and the engine gives an ear-splitting whine.

Jeb's fingers are forced from the splintered wood on the wheel, and he sails through the air and strikes the metal siding of the cabin. The cruiser splashes into the greenish-brown water, sending cold spray over the decking. Jeb's back aches, and blood is trickling onto his cheek from a thin cut above his right eye. Scotty's clothes are drenched with red-and-brown streaks. He is motionless against the cabin. His eyes are open and distant.

Jeb struggles along the slippery floor and places his hand on Scotty's neck. No pulse. Jeb pulls his hand away from Scotty's neck, and it is covered in a deep-red liquid. Jeb shakes his head, wiping his hands on Scotty's shirt. Before Jeb can get to his feet, the cruiser begins listing to the port side. Jeb can hear the water rushing into the cabins below. On the deck, glass and torn metal slide across the surface.

Jeb scrambles to the starboard side. The red speedboat and the green speedboat race around Jeb's disabled and swiftly sinking vessel. The circling boats make two passes, and the damaged boat rocks slowly in the wake. "We know you're there!" a deep voice calls, cutting through the sound of rushing water. "Come on out. We will make this as painless as possible."

Jeb holds on to the post of the railing as the boat's starboard side lifts higher out of the water. Jeb sees a man with long blond hair and tan leathery skin holding a semiautomatic rifle. He has a lit cigar between his teeth. "You don't have much time left. Your boat will be at the bottom of the river in a few minutes." Cigar Man says through a cloud of smoke.

Jeb isn't giving himself over to these guys. They would shoot him and conveniently dispose of him. Nobody would ever find his body.

Jeb looks around frantically. His backpack hangs by its strap on the helm. Between the backpack and the helm, he sees the wooden grip of his revolver. If he's going out, he's going to take cigar man with him. Jeb slides along the wood flooring and plants his feet on the edge of the helm. He quickly grabs the gun and holds it tightly in his right hand with his finger on the trigger. He pulls the pack from the broken wood and slings it over his left shoulder.

He steps along the slippery inclined surface toward the rear of the boat. He sees the white-and-red boat rocking with the wake. He catches the other boat drifting along the other side. Jeb drops and crawls toward the rear as a fresh burst of gunfire fills the air. *Thunk, Thunk, Thunk.* Jeb clings to the wooden railing and swings his legs onto the small metal grate affixed to the boat. He takes a last look and lowers himself onto the grate. The water splashes onto his shoes.

Jeb feels the boat bend under his feet as it lists farther into the water. The cabin cruiser is almost on its side, and it is sinking more rapidly. Jeb looks quickly at the bank that is roughly thirty yards from the sinking vessel. He can make that, easy. He will need to stay hidden from his pursuers.

He shoves the gun in his pack and secures the bag to his body. "Time to go," Jeb whispers. As the step sinks into the murky brown water, Jeb takes a deep breath and lowers himself into the cool current. The current pulls him toward the bow of the boat. He kicks wildly downward, making sure he stays hidden below the sediment-filled river. Jeb can hear the boards on the cabin cruiser breaking under the force of the water.

Jeb's lungs burn, and his chest aches as he pushes himself forcefully through the churning water. He has been underwater for a minute already, and he can see tiny bursts of light in front of his clenched eyelids. *I have to be getting closer*, he thinks as he kicks his legs again and again. His muscles feel like they are on fire, and his chest feels like it is ready to explode. Jeb has never held his breath longer than a minute and a half before.

He passes the two-minute mark, and his pace slows. The river pulls him downstream as his muscles fail to keep up with the force of the water. He's not going to make it. This isn't the way he wanted to leave this earth.

As he prepares to let the confined air out of his chest, his feet hit something mushy. His feet sink into the thick mud of the riverbank. Jeb emerges from the cool water. The warm air strikes his lungs as he takes in a few deep breaths. He looks out at the sinking vessel with the two motorboats circling the last remnants that remain above the water.

Jeb is thirty yards downstream, and he crawls cautiously from the water into a thicket of reeds. He sits motionless in the muddy water as flies and mosquitoes swarm around his face. Jeb grabs a handful of mud and smears the cool, thick, blackish-brown clay onto his face and arms. This will help him stay hidden and also keep the pests from biting his skin. The reeds sway in the breeze in front of him. Jeb has his eyes trained on the circling speed boats. The cabin cruiser is fully submerged in the river, and he watches as they pull the body of Captain Scotty from the water. The men throw the lifeless form onto the deck of the boat.

Jeb sinks lower into the water as the boats rev their engines and begin making larger arcs around the sunken wreck. Jeb knows they are searching for him, since he didn't come to the surface with Scotty. Jeb takes another handful of mud and cover his head with the thick, earthy substance. It flows across his face and down his back. His face is the only part of his body above the waterline, and he is hidden by the thick stalks of the cattails.

The red-and-white speedboat races along the shore, and the man with long hair looks intently at the wooded slopes. As the boat nears his location, Jeb narrows his eyes so the whites don't draw attention. He holds his breath as the boat slows and the man looks toward the thick growth of cattails. *Move along*, Jeb thinks as he counts in his head, *seven, eight, nine . . .*

The man shoulders his rifle and looks through the scope north and south along the bank.

Twenty, twenty-one . . .

The green speed boat comes to a stop beside the red boat. "Anything?" the pilot yells.

"No, nothing." the man with long hair replies, still scanning the ridges.

"He's probably still in the cabin." the other man replies.

Thirty-five, thirty-six . . .

"Stram wants this cleaned up today." Long Hair says as he lowers the rifle and surveys the riverbank again.

"If he's dead, mission accomplished."

"I want to be sure," Long Hair says. "Stram will leave us in the bottom of the river if this guy is still alive."

The boats are twenty yards from Jeb's location, and they roll with the current. Suddenly, there is a deep throttling sound coming from upstream: "The gorge is a pristine site along the Tennessee River where bald eagles roam freely," an excited voice says over a loud speaker.

Jeb watches the men as they hurriedly stow their guns and quickly cover Captain Scotty's body.

The man in the green boat salutes Long Hair and opens the throttle, speeding downstream. Long Hair takes a last look at the riverbank as the *Tennessee Wildlife Cruiser* rumbles toward them.

Sixty, sixty-one . . .

Finally, Long Hair pushes the throttle forward and speeds away, sending a spray of water toward the shore. Jeb quietly lets out the burning air in his lungs and takes a deep, welcoming breath. He has never been happier to see a boat full of bird watchers than he is now. Jeb's eyes follow Long Hair until he turns the bend of the river. Jeb slowly emerges from the sticky, thick mud and pulls himself onto the shore. He lays on the soft green grass for a few minutes, and the muscles in his legs and arms twitch.

Jeb rolls onto his back and stares at the white clouds rolling across the sky. "Who is Stram?" Jeb breathes as he climbs to his feet. He has plenty of time to dwell on the answer as he starts the long walk to his car.

CHAPTER 8

Secrets

The downtown district of Camden is quiet at eight o'clock on a Monday evening. Jeb is standing under a bright marquee with flashing lights. Bright golden letters at the top of the sign let everyone in Camden know this block of Market Street belongs to "Fitzhume's." Fitzhume's is the period hangout for people who like big band music and swing dancing. Most of the other places in downtown Camden are quiet at this hour, but Fitzhume's is busy all the time.

Jeb checks his watch as he looks up and down the boulevard. A group of chattering women in their twenties flutter toward the door dressed like they were pulled from an F. Scott Fitzgerald novel. The sequins on their short dresses reflect the lights from the marquee. A tall, thin man wearing a pinstripe suit is standing beside a thick wooden door. Baz is the doorman for Fitzhume's, and his deep baritone voice fills the air. "Welcome to Fitzhume's. This your first time?"

The women laugh.

"Come on in, ladies. Have a wonderful experience."

Baz opens the door, and the women laugh and chatter as they enter.

"Hey, you coming in tonight, Strauss?" Baz yells as he allows another group of women to pass through the door.

Jeb shrugs his shoulders and walks toward the towering doorman. "Baz, you know I can't miss a night when the Julian Day Orchestra is playing." The Julian Day Orchestra is a big band like Glenn Miller, and their fast-track tunes take you back to a bygone era. Jeb never misses a Julian Day show at Fitzhume's unless he's away on business.

Baz raises his eyebrows. "You weren't here Friday, Saturday, or Sunday."

Jeb shakes his head. "Business this weekend, but hey, I'm here now."

Baz extends his large hand, and Jeb shakes it. "You came on a good night, brother," Baz says, winking. "Plenty of ladies in the house."

Jeb shakes his head and smiles. "Just the music for me, Baz."

Baz peers at him with his chin stuck out. "Okay, okay," Baz says. "Enjoy the show." Baz opens the door, and Jeb steps toward it.

Jeb stops and places his hand on the golden

handle. He looks up and down the street making sure he isn't being followed. ""

Baz scratches his freshly shaved chin for a second. "Something wrong?"

Jeb shakes his head. "No, but in my line of work you can never be too careful." That is a good thing. He doesn't want to meet up with the goons who tried to kill him when he's trying to relax. He tried contacting Margaret, but she has suddenly disappeared. Between the river incident and Margaret, he wants a night where he can enjoy himself.

Jeb steps from the street into a bright and noisy ballroom. It is like being transported from 2022 to 1928. Julian Day is standing in front of a group of musicians. He pulls on his trombone as it is pointing in the air. The beginning notes of "Chattanooga Choo-Choo" fills the room. Couples hurry to the large dance floor in front of the stage and begin twirling to the music.

Jeb walks slowly toward the back of the room to his favorite table. He takes a seat and watches Julian swing the horn right, then left. Jeb likes the slow melody of "Chattanooga Choo-Choo." He taps his foot to the beat as the band plays on.

"Would you like something to drink?" a brunette with a bob hairstyle asks with a wink.

"Ginger ale, please." Jeb replies.

"Nice choice, Mr. Strauss." she answers.

Jeb looks at her, and her beaming face lights up this corner of the dark ballroom. He studies her, trying to remember her name, but it just isn't coming into his mind.

Her lips curl at the corner of her mouth into a half smile. "What? You don't recognize me with the new do?" she says as she bounces her hair in her palm.

"How could I forget?" Jeb says, shaking his head. "Forgive me, Charlotte."

Charlotte has been at the club since Jeb started coming down to hear the big bands. She is always jovial and interested in what he is doing. Jeb is usually the youngest guy in the place, and he figures it is a way to break the monotony of slinging drinks to older patrons. "No worries," Charlotte says cheerfully. "Let me get this for you, and then you can tell me all about what you have been up to."

Jeb nods, and Charlotte hurries away. The band finishes the song, and the ballroom is filled with loud applause. Jeb claps softly as he watches the stage.

Julian Day steps to the microphone. "Thank you all for coming out tonight. It is so good to see so many fans dancing and moving to the beats of swing," Julian says in a southern drawl. "This music is special, and we thank you for still enjoying some the best music ever made." The crowd cheers louder, and a broad smile spreads across Julian Day's face. "Alright, Let's see if you all know this one," Julian says jubilantly. He takes his trombone and positions it close to his mouth. He turns and waves his arms to the horn section, and all the players place their instruments to their mouths. The band starts playing "Pennsylvania 6-5000," and as the members sway to the music, the dance floor fills with partners gliding across the smooth, polished wood.

Jeb scans the floor as the dancers rotate effortlessly. It is like they are levitating across the surface. As Jeb surveys the band and their motions, a woman sits at his table. He glances at her. "Nice to see you again, Margaret," he says as he drums the bass line of the music with his fingers on the table. "Sorry about your friend, Scotty."

Charlotte walks by quickly and places his drink on the table. She turns quickly and walks away in a huff. Jeb can see she is a little annoyed that there is another woman sitting at his table. He grasps the glass and slowly brings the crystal-clear container to his lips. "You could have told me that whatever is at the bottom of the river is so thoroughly protected," Jeb says calmly. He takes a long sip of the brown liquid as he watches the fine-tuned choreography of the band. They swing their trumpets and trombones in unison, and the ballroom is filled with vibrant brass sounds intermingled with bass and drums.

Jeb places the glass on the table and turns toward Margaret. Her face is blank as she watches the band play. "I'm sorry," she says absently. "I thought you could handle yourself." Her head turns, and her bright-green eyes are laser-focused on him. "I seem to have chosen the wrong man for the job," says Margaret sternly.

Jeb stares into her harsh eyes. He grabs his glass again and sips the warm liquid. He isn't taking the bait. "Maybe you did," Jeb replies coldly. He decides to go on the offensive in this conversation. "You don't seem too broken up over your friend dying. I know if it were me, I would be." Jeb downs the rest of his drink and places the glass delicately on the table as he keeps his eyes trained on her.

"Scott knew the dangers when I sent him to meet you," Margaret says coldly. "It is unfortunate."

"Unfortunate?" Jeb grumbles loudly. "A man is dead, and I almost joined him!" Jeb's anger is building. Being shot at and almost drowned tends to do that to people.

Margaret's face is blank, and her eyes are penetratingly focused. She shrugs her shoulders. "You're looking for lost treasure. You had to know others would be after it as well.," she says harshly.

Jeb wishes he had another drink on the table so he could settle himself. How can a person be so cold and unfeeling? "I didn't think there would be people ready to kill me for looking," Jeb replies, his voice rising.

"I told you that all knowledge of the *Baron* had been cleaned from the record," Margaret replies softly. She studies Jeb's face. "Why would that be? You are a smart man, Mr. Strauss. Can you not solve the riddle?"

"You knew there was going to be this much heat," Jeb shoots back a little too loud.

The lady sitting at the table beside his looks at

him.

"I don't think I want this job anymore," Jeb says through clenched teeth.

Margaret turns and watches the band playing on stage. "So be it," she says robotically.

Jeb is speechless. This whole episode is bizarre. He only wanted to enjoy some music, collect his thoughts, and formulate a new plan. Unfortunately, Margaret found him and ruined his night.

After a few moments of silence, Margaret stands. Jeb hadn't noticed her black dress when she sat down. The fine fabric forms to her body perfectly, and the dark material contrasts with her pale skin. "Good night, Mr. Strauss," Margaret says, not looking at him. She starts to walk away, but Jeb stands.

What am I doing? he thinks. Jeb wants to know what else is in the *Baron*. They aren't killing people to protect a gold shipment, that is for sure. What else is in the cargo hold of the vessel? Those men who broke into his boat and killed Scotty are killers. Jeb doesn't know who they work for, but if the government wiped away all documentation of the Baron, the government might be involved. CIA, FBI, or NSA. Could be any number of the alphabet-soup groups of the government.

Jeb steps in front of Margaret and holds his hands up, palms facing her. "Wait," he says calmly. "I want to find the *Baron*. I want to help you get whatever you're looking for."

She stares at Jeb with her cold, penetrating eyes. Jeb doesn't trust her to be forthcoming with information, but knowing that the government wants this part of history to remain hidden piques his interest. If he can get by Long Hair, maybe he will find what is lost. Jeb hopes he doesn't get filled with holes in the process.

"Let's enjoy the rest of Julian Day's show and talk about plans for bringing up the *Baron*," Jeb says, smiling.

"Very well," Margaret replies coldly.

Julian Day and the orchestra play "I've Got a Gal in Kalamazoo." The ballroom is filled with dancers, and the other patrons bob their heads to the beat. Jeb sits with a smile on his face as the music flows over him. There is nothing better in the world than Glenn Miller on a Monday night. The blare of the horns drowns the apprehension of Jeb's current assignment. At least for tonight, he can push work out of his mind.

*****

Jeb and Margaret walk along the riverfront under a bright whiteish moon. The cascading colors are a similar tone to Margaret's skin. Jeb has noticed her pale beauty, but seeing her under a full moon draws out the purity of her skin.

The reflection of the moon ripples across the flowing river. A few barges filled with crushed limestone drift silently on the dark water, and the sloshing water strikes the rocks along the shore. A young couple holding hands and giggling walks by them, obviously on a first date.

"Would you mind telling me what I am actually looking for?" Jeb asks.

Margaret is silent for a few seconds. "Like I told you, it is a family heirloom," Margaret replies coldly.

Jeb laughs in disbelief. "I don't think the alphabet squad are killing people over a family relic," Jeb replies. "If I had to make a guess, I would bet it is something they hope never sees the light of day again." Jeb glances at her, trying to see if there is a crack in her cold, stony demeanor.

Margaret's face is blank, and her bright-green eyes search his face.

Jeb waits but she doesn't respond. "The government is going to keep your heirloom hidden forever," Jeb continues.

Margaret stops walking and grabs his arm. "There are secrets in our past that are too arduous to bear. My great-great-grandfather ruined his name for a cause he believed in. He performed his duty as an officer, and what did they do with such loyalty? They cast him away and pretended he never existed. All because he was carrying their secret." Margaret looks at the moon, and she squeezes his arm in her strong grip.

Jeb isn't sure if he can believe her or if this is an act to get him on her side.

"I want his reputation restored, and I want the men in charge to pay for their crimes," Margaret says softly.

"What secret was he protecting?" Jeb asks.

"The contents of the crates weren't just gold shipments. There were dispatches and weapons that only a select few knew about," Margaret says.

" 'Weapons'?" Jeb replies exasperatedly.

"Weapons that used the forces of earth. Powerful weapons that have not been seen since biblical times. Weapons that are truly deplorable," Margaret replies.

"So you're telling me that your great-great-grandfather was running guns on the Tennessee River during the war."

"How have you ever found treasure?" she replies harshly. "Look. What my ancestor described were forces from the ground that, when amplified, can cause absolute destruction. Have you ever heard of the walls of Jericho?"

"You're kidding," Jeb replies, shaking his head.

"These weapons are real and so terrible that the government is keeping them safely submerged inside the *Baron*," Margaret scowls.

"Okay, so Ulysses Grant had access to a death ray or something that could topple a fortified city," Jeb spits back.

Margaret places her hands on her hips and

narrows her eyes. "This isn't a joke, Mr. Strauss," Margaret says sternly. "I want the proof! I want to prove my great-great grandfather served his country honorably. I want to restore his good name."

Jeb nods. "You also want to stick it to the feds," Jeb replies, raising his eyebrows.

"They did ruin our family name," Margaret replies. "They took our honor, and for that, their secrets are going to be revealed."

Jeb smiles as he touches her hand. "I think I know the general area where the *Baron* went down. With those goons patrolling upstream and downstream, it could be problematic surveying on the river," Jeb says.

Margaret looks at him sternly.

"But I have a friend who owes me a favor. He will fly me over the river so I can get readings."

"You think you can find it?" Margaret says.

"Precisely," Jeb says, winking.

"When you go to bring it up, I want to be there," Margaret says forcefully.

"I figured," Jeb says, smiling. "How can I say no?"

Jeb scans the area around them. He gets a feeling the people Long Hair works for are out there somewhere. He doesn't see anyone other than him and Margaret along the riverfront. Jeb grabs Margaret's hand and leads her toward the river district of Camden. It is time to get home. Jeb needs to call Clem and get an idea of when he can take Jeb up for an aerial survey.

He checks the time on his Marathon diver's watch. It is 12:10 a.m. He will wait until tomorrow to call Clem. Jeb looks at Margaret. "How did you like Julian Day?" Jeb asks.

"Who?" Margaret replies.

Jeb laughs. "You're all business."

Margaret glances at him as they walk along the rolling river. "It is easier that way," Margaret replies.

Jeb nods his head as they continue in silence under the bright-white moon.

CHAPTER 9

Paper Wings

The first rays of sunlight filter across the glassy water as Jeb pulls his paddleboard onto the deck of his houseboat. He leans his paddle against the Adirondack chair and pulls his saturated shirt over his head. The purple-and-brown bruises on his ribs have faded, but they still are painful.

Today is a busy day. Jeb must call Clem and convince him to fuel up his plane and take Jeb on a mapping excursion. He hopes Clem is still in town after their last take. Maybe Clem will have gold fever and want another score. Jeb snatches his notebook from the table and turns through the pages. "Time to find Captain Armstrong," Jeb says. He pulls on his cargo pants and stuffs the book in the side pocket. He slips on a shirt and socks, and pulls on his boots.

Jeb grabs his phone and keys, and climbs onto

the gangplank. He walks quickly toward his Saab. He doesn't want to see Calvin this morning. He doesn't want to discuss safe careers. Jeb opens the car door and falls into the seat. He places the key in the ignition, and the car comes to life. Jeb looks at his phone, searching for Clem's name.

Jeb dials his colleague, and the phone beeps as he waits. On the fifth ring, Clem's angry, grumbling voice blares through the earpiece. "What do you want?"

"Checking to see if you're available," Jeb asks.

"Not for you," Clem grumbles.

"Come on. Where is your sense of adventure?" Jeb shoots back.

"After the last one, I'm all adventured out," Clem snorts.

"Would thirty million change your mind?" Jeb replies.

Clem splutters and coughs through the headset as something crashes. It sounds like Clem dropped a set of symbols on a drum set. Jeb chuckles as another round of bangs comes through the receiver. Jeb waits a few seconds, "You all right, Clem?"

Clem coughs loudly. "Did you say 'thirty million'?" Clem say, sounding out of breath.

"Yep," Jeb replies smoothly.

"I need time to think," Clem splutters.

"This one should be an easy one," Jeb lies.

Jeb isn't about to tell Clem about the government agents killing anyone who gets too close to the treasure. He isn't going to tell him about the weapons, the conspiracy, and the overall general danger built into this endeavor. Jeb needs Clem to fly the plane so Jeb can get electromagnetic data on that area of the Tennessee River. Flying will be the only way to explore, with Long Hair and his henchman patrolling.

"I promise, it won't be like last time," Jeb continues.

"I still need time."

"How about millions of dollars," Jeb says confidently. "Just think about what you can do with half."

Jeb can hear the heavy breaths coming from the phone. He knows Clem will agree. That is a lot of money, and Clem is a true capitalist. The seconds tick by as Jeb waits. He has him now. After another few moments, Clem clears his throat. "What do you need?"

Jeb smiles. Today is starting out very well.

"I will need an aerial survey of a stretch of the Tennessee River. The part we are studying is a place known as the Suck. Interesting section of the river," Jeb says hurriedly.

"You paying for the gas?" Clem asks.

"It will come out of your cut," Jeb bristles.

"Fine," Clem grumbles. "When you wanting to go up?"

"I was thinking about this morning," Jeb replies.

"Can't do it that soon. Might be able to this

afternoon."

"You got a pressing engagement?" Jeb asks.

"Have to get to the airport and get the plane ready, buddy," Clem says.

Jeb closes his book and throws it on the passenger seat. He needs to get his gear ready, as well. He will need the magnetic receiver and the transmitter. "You be ready by 2 p.m.?" Jeb questions.

Clem lets out a burst of air. "That will be pushing it."

Jeb smiles. "I believe in you, Clem." Jeb chortles. "I will be at the airport at two. See you then." Jeb presses the End button on the phone and throws it on top of the field book.

He shoves the car into gear and slams on the gas. The tires spin in the loose gravel, kicking a cloud of dust out behind the car. He pulls onto the main road with a squeal of the tires and speeds off toward Camden.

*****

Jeb drives at the posted thirty-five-mile-per-hour speed limit along the tree-lined streets of the college. He is stopping by the geology department to borrow the survey equipment he will need to conduct his field study. He probably should buy his own, considering his last haul, but Jeb has become friends with some of the professors in the geology department. He likes coming over and getting their opinions about the data he has gathered.

He particularly likes Dr. Rock Wilson. Rock Wilson is a geologist who likes using electromagnetism to locate hidden relics. The last time Jeb came to campus, Rock and his colleagues were setting out on an expedition to see if his magnetoscope could detect fluctuations in the magnetic fields created by Earth. Rock believed his device could be used to explain why the pyramids were built where they are in Egypt. Why the pre-Columbian civilizations built their vast cities and temples at their locations. If it worked, his magnetoscope could revolutionize the fields of archeology, history, and geology.

Jeb hopes they are around this morning. Neither Rock nor Dr. Mies gives him trouble when he wants to borrow the transmitter and receiver. They only want to hear about the survey plan, and they offer advice on how to better plot a grid. As long as Dr. Sims isn't around. The head of the department is a boorish, arrogant, and rude individual who doesn't like anyone in the department—or their friends.

Jeb parks in front of a single-story brick building with a glass front door. The sign on the door lets everyone know this is the building for the Geology and Paleontology departments. Bruschi Hall is small compared to the other grand brick buildings on campus. It is like the college views the geologic sciences as inferior to the other disciplines.

He collects his phone and his book, and steps out of the car. The air is thick and humid. His shirt instantly sticks to his body. He walks toward the glass front door. Maybe Dr. Wilson will be here and he will tell Jeb about the trip to New Mexico.

Jeb opens the door, and the cool, dry air from inside strikes his body. It is a refreshing coolness, and he hurries inside.

The inside is lit with fluorescent lights that buzz loudly. Jeb walks to the receptionist's desk, where a man with shaggy blond hair is sitting reading a minerology book. "Hey, Gil," Jeb says.

Gil looks over the top of the book. "Jeb Strauss. How are you doing, man?"

"Not too bad—just trying to stay busy," Jeb replies.

"You on a new treasure hunt?" Gil asks.

"Maybe. Is Dr. Wilson around?" Jeb says.

"You didn't hear?" Gil says in a hushed voice.

"Didn't hear what?" Jeb replies, eyebrows raised.

"He didn't come back," Gil whispers.

"He left the university?" Jeb asks incredulously.

Gil looks around the office, obviously making sure no one is around. "He disappeared on his expedition in New Mexico," Gil whispers.

Jeb shakes his head in disbelief. How could Dr. Wilson disappear? He is very thorough in his approach, and he is resourceful. "Any ideas where he is?" Jeb asks.

Gil shakes his head. "Sims came back very angry. Said that Dr. Wilson and Dr. Mies were careless and their research was a threat to the lives of their department members. He also said their research was a threat to this university," Gil whispers.

That doesn't seem right. Jeb will need to look into this when he has more time. He has a pressing engagement of finding a boatload of gold entombed in the sediments of the Tennessee River. "Dr. Sims isn't around, is he?" Jeb says with a grimace.

Gil looks over his shoulder. "Not today, but you never know when he is going to pop in," Gil replies.

"Is anyone from the team around today?" Jeb asks.

"Dr. Milner is in," Gil replies.

"Dr. Mies or Dr. Brown?" Jeb questions.

"Dr. Mies is at home resting, and Dr. Brown is out for a few days."

It looks like it has to be Dr. Milner—or leaving without the survey equipment. Jeb might be purchasing his own setup to keep this from happening in the future. He looks around the room, with its samples of rocks under glass containers. Jeb has only talked with Dr. Milner a few times, and that was while he was visiting Dr. Brown. Jeb isn't sure Dr. Milner will let him borrow the university's expensive research material, but he needs the detectors. "Yeah. Let me see Milner," Jeb says.

Gil picks up the phone and dials. "Yes, Jeb

Strauss is here to see you," Gil says into the handset. Gil nods and places the phone into its cradle. "You know where his office is?"

Jeb nods. He walks down the hallway. There are cabinets filled with fossils and rocks. At the end of the long hallway is a weathered wooden door with a plastic nameplate hanging askew beside it. Jeb taps lightly on the door, and the nameplate shifts farther down the wall. Being the youngest professor in the Geology department obviously has its drawbacks. "Come in!" booms a voice from the other side of the door.

Jeb opens the door and steps into a warm, dry room with a small desk fan rotating and rustling the papers neatly stacked on the desk. Dr. Milner is a young blond-haired Australian with a PhD in sedimentation. "Mr. Strauss, it is good to see you again." Dr. Milner smiles. "Have a seat."

Jeb sits in the worn office chair, with its peeling armrests.

"What can I do for you?" Milner asks.

Jeb surveys the large rocks on the shelf behind Dr. Milner. There is a large slab of sandstone with perfect bedding planes, and there is a perfect plant fossil beside it. It looks like it was taken from the same rock.

"I need to borrow the lidar setup for a survey I am conducting," Jeb says, smiling.

"I can't let you have that," Milner says, shaking his head.

"I will have it back to you in better condition

than I take it out of here," Jeb replies imploringly.

"What are you surveying?" Milner questions.

"That is classified at the moment, but I can assure you the equipment will be cared for as if it were my own."

"Does Dr. Brown let you use the university's property?"

Jeb looks at the Australian, eyes narrowed.

Dr. Milner rubs his chin between his fingers as he stares at Jeb.

Jeb smiles and shrugs his shoulders. "It is all part of research. Dr. Wilson lets me use the devices, and he interprets the data." Jeb winks.

Dr. Milner rubs his hands together. "And you want me to grant the same permissions that were given in the past?"

Jeb laughs. "You sound so formal. We are all friends here. We are all on the same side. We are all searching for the truths of the past," Jeb says, folding his hands in his lap. Jeb studies Dr. Milner's face, waiting for the formal response to be replaced with a youthful thirst for discovery.

The Australian smiles. "Don't let Dr. Sims know I am helping you."

Jeb holds his right hand over his heart. "You have my word."

Dr. Milner opens his desk and extracts a set of keys. "Is this about treasure?" Dr. Milner says, eyebrows rising.

Jeb shrugs and looks away.

"You are starting to get a name for yourself

in the treasure-finding community," Dr. Milner continues. "I have read a few stories."

Jeb laughs. "Those are just stories. Embellishments."

Dr. Milner studies him for a few seconds. He stands. "Let's get the lidar."

Jeb stands and follows Dr. Milner out of the office.

*****

Jeb pulls into the Camden Regional Airport, which isn't much of an airport. It has one landing strip and a small tower. There is a small single-engine plane racing down the runway and slowly rising into the air. Jeb drives along the access road toward the hangers in the distance. Jeb hopes Clem is set for the flight. Jeb is early, but he figures that even if Clem is running behind him, being here ready to go might cause Clem to work faster.

Jeb parks his Saab in a spot beside the white metal door of the smallest hanger. He throws the door open and steps out into the sticky, oppressive heat of Camden. Sweat immediately trickles down his face, and he wipes it away with his hand. Jeb grabs the plastic case with the lidar inside, locks up the car, and walks into the shade of the vast building.

Clem is standing beside his red-and-white Cessna 172, looking into the motor compartment.

Jeb coughs loudly.

Clem looks at him and rolls his eyes. "You're early," Clem grumbles.

Jeb places the black case beside the plane. "Just a few minutes. Besides, I thought I might give you a hand," Jeb says jovially.

Clem continues turning a wrench without looking up from his work.

"Okay," Jeb says, "I will attach this to the plane, and we will be all set when you are finished with your preparations."

Clem shakes his head. "Don't put any holes in my plane," Clem snarls.

Jeb holds his hands out in a *Would I do that?* response.

Jeb opens the black box and removes the first transmitter from its foam enclosure. He removes the attachment brackets and takes the gear to the wing of the plane. Jeb holds the transmitter to the wing stabilizer and bolts the device to the wing. After a few minutes of repositioning and tightening, the first transmitter is ready for action. Jeb activates the transmitter. The machine beeps three times and a red light flashes on the top of the black box.

Jeb grabs the other piece of electrical equipment and attaches it to the other wing. Once it's affixed to the wing, Jeb initiates the program to receive the transmissions from both transmitters. The receiver beeps, and Jeb opens his laptop and starts the lidar's software app. As he waits for the app to run a full diagnostic on the system, Jeb checks his watch. Almost two o'clock.

The program shows eighty-nine percent complete. Jeb sets the laptop and the receiver in the cabin of the plane. Clem closes the engine compartment and stows his wrench in his pocket. He walks around the plane, examining the wings and the tail, running his fingers along the surface. Jeb hops in the seat and delicately places the computer on his legs. "Time to find the gold, Clem!" Jeb yells as he bangs his hand on the roof of the cabin.

Clem grumbles something inaudible from the rear of the plane as Jeb continues pounding on the walls. Clem throws the door open to the cockpit and glares at Jeb. "This is *my* plane, not yours," Clem says through clenched teeth. "I am doing you a favor."

Jeb slowly lowers his hand and releases his fist. A smiles spreads across Jeb's face. "Let's make some magic happen," Jeb says enthusiastically.

Clem grumbles something else inaudible and climbs into the cockpit. Clem motions toward a man with a small gas-powered cart. The man jumps from the cart and attaches a lead to the front of the plane. The man pulls the plane from the hanger out into the bright sunshine.

Clem places a pair of thick sunglasses over his eyes. They look like ski goggles. Jeb thinks about questioning his form of eyewear, but thinks it could push his friend over the edge. He needs this airplane ride if he ever hopes of conducting the survey of the Tennessee River. Jeb bites his lip and slips on a pair of Ray-Bans. Every time he flies with Clem, Jeb always brings his aviator glasses. He isn't an aviator, but he likes to look the part.

The engine starts, and the propeller spins. Clem rolls the plane forward. "Tower, this is Red Ryder One," Clem says slowly. "Ready for takeoff."

There is a crackle from the headset. "You're clear for takeoff."

The plane rolls onto the runway and moves toward the end of the strip of smooth concrete. The plane turns and begins picking up speed. It races toward the end of the wide runway, and Clem pulls back on the controls. The planes shutters as the wheels lose contact with the ground.

Jeb yells, "*YEEEEEEHAAAWWWWW!*" as the plane soars into the blue sky.

"Why do you have to do that every time?" Clem says, looking exhausted.

"Just channeling Howling Mad Murdoch," Jeb says, winking. Jeb laughs as he looks out the window into a vast expanse of endless sky. The thought of finding the *Baron* swims swiftly into his mind. Jeb remembers what Margaret told him about the weapon that remains hidden with the old steamship, safely entombed from the public in the sediments of the Tennessee River. What does it look like? How big is it? Is it the size of a Howitzer shell, or is it something the size of a laptop? Will the lidar pick up the signature of whatever it is that was used to destroy cities and armies? He chuckles. Focus on the gold. That is what you are after, he thinks as he looks out the window

Jeb has more questions than answers, and that is something he doesn't like. He likes knowing. He painstakingly researches the quests he conducts so he has all the T's crossed and I's dotted. This time, nothing is concrete. Nothing is absolute. The information about the *Baron* isn't absolute. He hopes the words from the diary are about the lost steamer. There is no other referenced information about the ship or the contents of its cargo. There is nothing available. The only clues he has are the descriptions from his client, Margaret Armstrong. Jeb doesn't trust her entirely. She is calculating and deceptive.

Jeb smiles as he looks out the window at the Tennessee River below, the brown water meandering through the countryside between tree-lined ridges. They have passed over Walden Ridge and are moving northwest toward the area known as the Suck.

"We are almost at your heading," Clem says robotically.

"Got it," Jeb replies, moving his arm like a robot.

"Ha ha," Clem responds. "Why do I take you places in my plane? I must be crazy."

"You are crazy. Just not in a good way." Jeb retorts laughing.

"Do you even know how to use that." Clem

points at the computer. "It looks a little too complicated for you.".".

Jeb presses the control panel that initiates the transmitters. The screen lights up, and a large red button flashes on the screen. "All is ready," Jeb replies, giving Clem a thumbs-up. "You might need to be a little lower though."

Clem smirks at Jeb as he angles the controls downward. "You *do* know I'm the pilot, right?" Clem replies.

Jeb salutes and points downward.

The plane flies over the dark ribbon of water. Jeb presses the Activate button, and the transmitters come to life, sending out beams toward the bending river below. Jeb is most interested in the portion of the river where the tributary of Suck Creek enters the channel. This is the section where many boats were lost in the past.

"Fly a normal grid pattern!" Jeb calls.

Clem nods and watches the horizon as the receiver blips and bloops in the cockpit. They fly over the intersection of the two rivers for thirty minutes, giving the lidar ample time to produce enough data. Jeb has his eyes fixed on his laptop screen when Clem taps him on the arm. "Looks like we got company, buddy," Clem says in a worried voice.

Jeb looks out the window, and three boats are circling under the airplane.

"Well, that took longer than I thought," Jeb says, shrugging his shoulders.

"You know these guys?" Clem questions.

"I don't *know* them, just know *about* them," Jeb says calmly.

"Oh no," Clem says as the color fades from his face. He pulls the stick to the right, and the plane banks hard.

Jeb grabs the computer before it smashes into the side of the compartment. Jeb sees a streak of red fly by the wing of the plane. "What w-was th-that?" Jeb stammers.

"That was a surface-to-air projectile!" Clem yells.

He pushes the stick forward, and the ground races toward them at a high rate of speed. The trees are so close that Jeb can see the individual leaves. Jeb's heart pounds as he grips his computer.

"They better not hit my plane, Jeb," Clem growls as he pulls the controls backward, causing the plane to cease its dive.

Jeb catches sight of another flare jetting toward them at a high rate of speed. "Clem! Incoming!" Jeb calls.

Clem quickly moves the plane to the right in a bank that causes the wings to skim the tree tops. "If they hit my plane, you are in serious trouble," Clem growls.

"Get us out of here, then!" Jeb yells as the flying stream of light passes in front of the cabin window. "Oh, jeez! That was close," Jeb continues.

"What do you think I'm doing?" Clem grimaces.

"Go that way," Jeb says, pointing to the ridge in

front of them. "If we can make it to the ridge, we're golden."

"Unless they have air support," Clem growls.

Jeb hadn't thought about jets being called in to erase them from existence.

The plane climbs higher, and the muscles in Clem's jaw tighten as he presses the throttle forward. The engine whines, and the cabin shudders as they climb toward the summit. Jeb watches the river behind them, waiting for the killing shot to hit. The engine sputters, and Jeb has a feeling the plane is about to stall. Jeb turns and sees Clem rocking backward and forward in the seat as he pushes the throttle forward. The engine comes to life, and it shoots the plane higher into the air. The craft levels and passes over the rocky precipice. Jeb can no longer see the river, and he throws his head back against the seat. They have escaped. He looks at Clem. "You are a better pilot than I give you credit for." Jeb smiles.

Clem snarls, "This isn't the time for such pleasantries."

Jeb nods slowly. "Fair enough. Too soon after a near-death experience," Jeb continues. He scans the blue sky around them, searching for aircraft that could make their lives a little less comfortable. Jeb holds his laptop tightly in his cold fingers as he watches the air intently. "How long until we make it back to the airport?" Jeb questions.

Clem looks at his watch. "ETA thirty minutes."

Jeb hopes nothing happens in those thirty

minutes. He wants a calm flight with no more surface-to-air missiles flying by the plane. This trip was almost a complete disaster. If they had hit the plane, the wings would have folded like paper and burned quickly.

After ten minutes, there are no other adversaries chasing them. Jeb opens his laptop and begins studying the data the aerial survey was able to produce. He hopes he has something. He hopes the outline of the *Baron* is plain and distinct. He hopes it is easily accessible. If it is buried in twenty feet of sediment, that could pose a problem. He doesn't have the means—or the desire—to file for the proper permits for an excavation of that size. The Tennessee authorities have made exploration in the river absolutely impossible with their current set of regulations. But if the *Baron* is in shallow enough water, Jeb can forgo the formalities and recover the wreck covertly.

CHAPTER 10

Bend in the River

J eb stands on the deck of the Kaiser with his laptop open. He takes a glass from the table next to him and downs the last remaining drops of sweet tea. Jeb wipes his mouth with the back of his hand and sets the glass on the table next to his .38 revolver. After all that has gone one, he feels much safer having his pistol with him at all times. Jeb never knows when Long Hair will come for another visit, and he wants to be ready when he sees Long Hair again.

Jeb looks at the setting sun as it falls behind the ridges west of Camden. The golden beams of light reflect off the greenish-brown water. The roar of a speed boat engine pierces the calmness of the sunset, and his houseboat rocks with the wake. Jeb watches the white boat barrel upstream, and he notices four ladies in their early twenties chattering and laughing. *That could be fun*, he thinks as the boat disappears from view.

Jeb looks at the computer screen, and there are multiple reds and yellows forming the outlines of boats hiding at the bottom of the river. Most of the wrecks are small. Jeb's analysis shows that the majority of the vessels submerged in the river are old flat-bottomed boats. Jeb ages the smaller wrecks as prior to steam power, so late 1700s through the early 1800s. Those are much older than what he is looking for. However, there is one large, more streamlined image in bright orange that appears to have a distinctive paddle wheel attached. This is the vessel Jeb will investigate.

The paddle-wheel steamer is the right age for being the *Baron*, and judging by the placement, it appears to be in the deeper part of the channel. Jeb smiles as he gazes at the screen. That means there isn't as much sediment on top of the vessel. This should be a much easier salvage operation than he ever thought possible. The only thing that presents a very imposing issue is the government agents guarding the wreck. That poses the greatest challenge to finding the treasure.

Jeb closes his laptop and stores it in his bag, along with his field book. He grabs the .38 from the table and places it delicately in his shoulder holster. It is time to procure everything he will need to retrieve the gold and the magic box of Captain Armstrong.

It takes Jeb until midnight to check his

diving gear to make sure it is in excellent working condition. He has four tanks fueled and ready to go. He has his lighting for the trip into the river. It will be dark, and the visibility only a few feet. That could be an issue, but he will need to wait until he is underwater to be sure. His four spotlights should provide the illumination needed at that depth.

There is a knock at the door. He checks his watch, nine o'clock. Jeb slowly walks toward the door, gripping the handle of his revolver. He moves the curtain aside, and standing in the pale glow from the front-door light is Margaret. She is wearing glasses and a long coat. Her pale skin radiates the bright white light. Jeb grabs the handle and opens the door. He searches the gangplank and the surrounding boats in the marina as he ushers her inside without a word.

"Thank you for calling," Margaret says as Jeb closes the door and bolts the lock.

Jeb turns "Can't be too careful."

"You have found it?" Margaret asks, pushing her glasses farther up her nose.

"That's why you're here." Jeb smiles. "You asked me to find the *Baron*, and that is what I've done."

"Can I see the images you talked about on the phone?" Margaret asks sternly.

Jeb walks to his table and pulls his computer from his bag. He quickly opens the laptop and searches through the images. Margaret is standing beside him, watching as different images flash on the screen. She rubs her chin between her finger and thumb. She glares at the image that has the bright orange and reds surrounded by deep blues and greens. "That is it?" she says, pointing to what looks like a paddle wheel.

"I believe it is," Jeb replies. "Perfect location too."

Margaret drums her fingers on the wooden table top as she stares absently at the bright screen. Jeb lays his field book beside the computer and points to the topographic map taped to the white page. "We can't use the river to get in and get out. Our Fed friends are draped over the area like a thick blanket," Jeb says, shaking his head.

"We can retrieve the boxes at night," Margaret replies robotically.

"That is what I am thinking," Jeb responds, rubbing the right side of his face. "We can sneak in, take what we want, and be gone before Long Hair and his goon squad realize." Jeb places his finger on the topographic map and looks at Margaret. "This is where we will start," Jeb says, eyes narrowed.

"That is a bit far to walk with gear and boxes we are salvaging," Margaret replies, rubbing her chin.

Jeb traces a small, dashed brown line that runs along the base of the ridge. Margaret watches as he moves his finger slowly. "I'm up for a nice hike," Jeb replies, smiling. "How much do you think this crate of yours weighs?"

Margaret looks intently at the screen. Her face

is expressionless, and it appears she is carefully formulating her response. "I cannot be sure, but from what information has been passed down through the family, it should weigh about thirty pounds."

Jeb grimaces and takes his field book and computer and stores them in his bag. He secures the bag and walks toward the window.

The bright moon casts a white glow on the slow-moving water. The houseboat gently rocks on the small ripples of the current. "We try tomorrow night," Jeb says calmly.

Margaret nods her head slowly. "You have everything ready?"

Jeb smiles. "I will need to convince a friend that I need his help again, but considering the payout, I don't think that will be an issue."

Margaret smiles. This is the first time Jeb has seen her harsh features soften. Her green eyes sparkle.

"Be here at nine, and we will be on our way," Jeb says.

Jeb watches the gray clouds drift across the face of the moon. He hopes for a smooth recovery, but with how his luck has been going lately, Jeb has an uneasy feeling. He touches the handle of his .38. At least he will be prepared when he meets Long Hair.

Margaret clears her throat behind him.

Jeb turns, slowly blinking. "Sorry," Jeb replies. "Thinking about the best way not to die tomorrow."

Margaret takes five long strides across the floor and stands in front of him. Her bright-green eyes bore into him. Her stern features return as she grabs his hand. "You are on the precipice of a great discovery," Margaret says calmly. "Do not fear the unknown."

Jeb looks away toward the window. Her words do little to combat the uneasiness of the venture, but he will be ready.

She releases his hand and walks toward the door. "I will see you tomorrow," Margaret says as she grabs the handle on the door. Without waiting for a response, she opens the door and walks out into the moonlit night.

Jeb strides across the living room and watches her walk to her car. "Let's see what happens," Jeb breathes as he watches the bright-red taillights of her car as she drives away.

*****

Jeb stands at the railing of his houseboat, he called Clem and he is ready for the excavation. A towboat blows its horn as it moves slowly along the river. The white towboat sprays the water ahead in bright beam of light from the large lamp. Jeb checks his watch, and a smile spreads across his face. Somebody is looking down on him with favor at the moment. That long, beautiful towboat will be getting to the bend in the river known as the Suck close to the time he will be excavating the wreck of the *Baron*. He contacted the towing company and told them that an archaeological investigation will be ongoing along the Tennessee River close to Suck Creek, and he wanted to know their time of arrival. The company had been very helpful by giving him their time. Jeb claps his hands together and grabs the two large black duffle bags at his feet.

He carries the heavy bags across the deck and places them delicately on the gangway. He grabs the railing and pulls himself up onto the wobbly platform. He surveys the dark surroundings and, satisfied that all is the way it should be, Jeb grabs his bags and carries them toward the parking lot. His revolver is cold against his skin as he walks slowly toward his Saab.

He steps from the wooden planking to the gravel of the parking lot. The rocks crunch under his feet, and that is the only sound, aside from the chirping of the cicadas. He watches the shadows around his car as he nears. His pulse quickens and sweat beads form on his brow. He flexes his fingers around the handle of the bag as he steps beside his car. He looks inside, searching the front seat and then the backseat. He lowers the bag in his right hand and slowly opens the back door.

He has his fingers around the handle of his revolver as he swivels on the spot, carefully looking into the darkness. During this month's tenants meeting, he plans to address the lack of lighting in the parking area. He slowly releases his grip on the pistol and grabs the bag at his feet. He places the duffle bag on the floor behind the driver's seat. He lays the other bag softly on the backseat.

Jeb has everything he will need for the retrieval tonight. He loads two sets of diving gear, high-powered spotlights, a retractable shovel, and his survey equipment. He checks his watch again, and as he looks up, the bright headlights of a car drive toward him. He takes a deep breath and instinctively grabs his .38. The car stops in front of him. He breathes a sigh of relief as Margaret steps out into the humid night. *I bet engineers have more relaxed evenings than I am having,*" Jeb thinks as he walks toward Margaret.

"Glad you didn't leave without me," Margaret says sternly.

"I thought about it." Jeb laughs. "Everything is ready to go."

Margaret carries a brown shoulder satchel. It looks like something an archaeologist carries to store their journals and writing devices. From the vibes Jeb gets from her, he bets there is a weapon of some kind hidden inside. As Jeb watches her glide around the front of the car, he notices her coolness. They are heading into the unknown tonight. A dangerous dive is on the horizon, along with the chance of meeting up with the men who killed Captain Scotty. That would make a normal person nervous. *He* is a little nervous, but Margaret is calm.

Jeb isn't sure what to make of it, but he doesn't have time to dwell on her psychological makeup. The trip to Suck Creek will take some time, and he wants to be onsite and ready when the barge rolls by. This should give them some cover.

Margaret opens the door and slides into the seat. "You coming?" she asks pointedly. Jeb shakes his head and hops into the driver's seat. He closes the door quickly and starts the car. "Time to find some treasure," he says, and he shoves the car into gear, slamming his foot on the gas. The car slides through the gravel, leaving a trail of dust behind it. As the tires hit the pavement, the car makes a barking sound and Jeb smiles. The smell of burning rubber fills the cabin of the car. He races through the deserted streets along the marina district, picking up speed as he nears the main highway.

The masts of the sailboats speed by the car as he passes the last marina. He steers onto Highway 41 and accelerates quickly up to sixty miles an hour. Jeb glances at Margaret as she taps her fingers lightly on her canvas bag. Jeb starts to ask what is in the bag, but decides the silence is needed. He can go over the plan he has in his mind a few more times. He wants to be well prepared when he makes it to Suck Creek. He wants all his actions to be so well rehearsed they are instinctual.

After driving in silence for an hour, Margaret turns and looks sternly at him. "This friend you have helping—is he trustworthy?" Margaret asks, eyebrows rising.

Jeb glances at her and, seeing her scowl, shakes his head. "I've worked with him several times, and though he whines a lot, he does very good work."

The muscles in Margaret's face tighten. "That isn't what I asked," Margaret says, clenching her jaw.

"Hey now," Jeb protests. "This is *my* operation. So no armchair quarterbacking. You got *me*." Jeb looks from the Margaret's angry face to the road. He drums his fingers on the steering wheel. "You're getting the legacy of Captain Armstrong, whatever that is, and I am getting the gold. It is a win-win for all of us," Jeb spits as he pushes the pedal down to the floor and the car accelerates.

Margaret looks out the window. "I'm sorry," she says hurriedly. "It's just, the closer we get to finding the crate, the more determined I become."

Jeb grips the wheel tightly as they move along the dark highway. "What are you going to do with the crate when you have it, if you don't mind me asking?" Jeb questions.

Margaret looks at him sternly, and her bright-green eyes appear more vibrant than he has ever seen them. "Like I said: I will restore the honor to our family." The words trail away, and Margaret becomes silent again. She is rigid and stares out the window.

Jeb ponders her words. How is she going to restore the honor to her family? If that box has in it what she believes, she will have a power that hasn't been seen in a long time—the power to destroy. Jeb doubts that whatever is in the crate destroyed

Jericho. How could it?

He grips the wheel tighter and goes through the plan again. His job is to retrieve the crate and the gold. The gold, he gets, and he's happy with that.

*****

Jeb pulls onto a dirt road off Highway 41. This is the access road that should take them along the base of the ridge to the point where Suck Creek enters the Tennessee River. It should be a five-minute drive along this bumpy pathway to get to their jump-off location. Jeb's heart beats faster as he drives the car in the center of the red-clay road. He checks his watch quickly. Their timing needs to be spot on if they want to use the barge as cover. Any slip ups could pose a problem in timing the barge's arrival.

He turns the headlights off and slows to five miles per hour. Up ahead, he can see a dark pickup truck parked on the side of the road. Jeb pulls behind the truck and turns the engine off. Clem flings the truck door open and holds his arms out wide. "You're late," Clem growls.

Jeb steps out of his Saab and holds his finger to his lips. "We are really close to the river," Jeb whispers. "We don't want to alert anyone to our presence."

Clem kicks a pebble into the silent pine trees along the road. "You should be here on time," Clem grumbles in a harsh whisper.

"Help me get the gear!" Jeb calls as he pulls a big duffle bag from the backseat. He hands the first bag to Clem.

Clem stares at Margaret as she sits quietly in the front seat. "Who is this?" Clem whispers.

Jeb glances toward the front as he wrestles the second bag from the floor of his car. "This is my client. Margaret, this is Clem. Clem, this is Margaret." Jeb replies hurriedly.

"Pleasure," Margaret says with a sigh.

Jeb holds the duffle bag in his right hand and his field book in his left. He studies the map on the page and points toward the distant ridge to the east. "Time to go," Jeb says.

Margaret slowly opens the door and pulls her satchel over her shoulder. She follows Jeb and Clem along a dark, narrow trail. The wind blows softly through the pines, and the rustling needles in the canopy mask their footfalls on the compact clay path.

After walking in silence for ten minutes, Clem hurries to walk beside Jeb. "This is a long hike to be carrying a few million in gold out of here," Clem whispers harshly.

Jeb can't see his face, but he is sure Clem is wearing his usual scowl before they find treasure. He is always the skeptic until they have a pocketful of loot.

"We will get all the treasure back," Jeb says defiantly.

"How much farther?" Clem grumbles.

"Just up ahead," Jeb replies. "Now be quiet. We don't want to attract any unwanted attention."

Clem grumbles something under his breath and falls in behind Jeb. Jeb wonders why he always brings Clem along—the price he has to pay for a pilot and plane. Clem does offset some of the danger. Most of the time the bad guys focus on him because of his size and that gives Jeb enough time to figure a way out of trouble. Maybe it is a selfish reason for including Clem, but so far it has worked out.

The trail ends, and in front of Jeb is a thick growth of privet. He pushes through the branches and steps out into the moonlit night. The white light reflects off the slow-moving water. Jeb motions for Clem and Margaret to move back into the thick undergrowth. The stand of privet will give them cover from anyone moving along the river.

Jeb delicately places his duffel bag on the soft bed of pine needles lying on the ground. He slowly unzips the bag and extracts the mask, regulator, and tank. Clem places the other bag beside the first, and Jeb unzips the bag and removes the other set of scuba gear.

"I'm not going down there," Clem hisses.

Jeb glares at Clem. "No need for you to worry. I'm taking someone who can do the job," Jeb whispers. Jeb looks at Margaret. "Are you ready for this?" Jeb asks.

Margaret walks over confidently and examines the regulator. She turns the equipment over in her hand. "Let's do this," Margaret says.

Jeb nods and pulls on his flippers. He attaches the lines and pulls the tank onto his back. He has the goggles sitting at the top of his head. "We just need to wait for the barge," Jeb breathes.

Margaret looks through the thick growth at the glistening water. "Looks like we are the only ones out here tonight," Margaret says. She glances upstream and downstream, obviously studying the surface of the water.

Jeb shakes his head. "We are sticking with the plan," he says. "They are out there, and I would rather find the wreck under the cover of that barge. Long Hair can't do anything as long as the barge is between us and them."

Margaret nods slowly as she keeps her eyes fixed on the river.

The soft gurgling of water flowing into the Tennessee River from Suck Creek mixes with the rustling of the leaves in the trees. The night is calm, and on any other night, Jeb would like to be sitting on his kayak or his paddleboard, drifting along with the current. The river is peaceful and relaxing, and Jeb goes there to collect his thoughts. Tonight, however, his pulse is elevated and a cool sweat forms on his brow. He wants this to go smoothly, but he knows Long Hair is out there in the darkness somewhere.

CHAPTER 11

Into the Darkness

The stillness of the night ends when a loud horn blares from upstream. Jeb watches as the searchlights from the towboat drift across the calm water. The barge drifts slowly toward them. Jeb looks at Margaret as he places the mask over his eyes. "Time to shine," Jeb says, smiling.

Margaret quickly pulls on her mask and installs the mouthpiece of her gear. She holds her light against her body, and steps from the darkness into cold brown water of the river. In an instant, she disappears into the drifting current.

Jeb turns to Clem. "Give us about thirty minutes," Jeb says.

Clem nods, and Jeb places his regulator in his mouth and drifts into the river.

The barge is fifty yards upstream from their

entry point. Jeb checks his watch and quickly dives into flowing river. The white light from the moon filters into the upper five feet of water. As Jeb swims deeper, the light disappears and a blackness envelops him. He switches his spotlight on and angles his body downward. The water grows colder as he moves into deeper water. Jeb is at thirty feet, and his bright-yellow light bounces off the heavy sediments suspended in the water. The current pulls on his body, dragging him down stream.

Jeb has calculated how far upstream he needed to be so he could drift to the wreck. He hopes he got it right. His spotlight illuminates the water, and he can see five feet ahead of him. Suddenly, a beam of light breaks through the blackness of the water. Margaret swims toward him, and she points down. Jeb nods. They both angle downward and kick their legs swiftly. Jeb checks his watch. They have been in the river for fifteen minutes. They should be getting close to the bottom.

This part of the river is seventy feet deep, and the lidar survey showed the paddle wheel of the *Baron* in the center of the channel. Jeb points the bright-yellow beam ahead, and dark objects drift into view from the shadows. Jeb's ears pulse, and he forces himself to slow his breathing. He doesn't want to run out of air before he reaches the wreck.

They continue downward, and the bright lights catch a circular structure protruding from the thick mud at the bottom of the river. Jeb's heart jumps as he kicks wildly toward the ancient relic.

Jeb shines his light on the surface of the object. It is reddish-brown, and Jeb scrapes flakes of rust from the metal. It's the paddle wheel. He looks at Margaret, and her green eyes are dancing behind her goggles. Jeb gives her a thumbs up, and he kicks his feet toward the center of the wreck.

A deep rumble passes slowly through the water, and it vibrates the sediments around the rusting wreckage. Small flakes of rust break free from the paddle wheel and drift swiftly on the current. Jeb breathes slowly as he places his hands on the rusty metal rings in the thick mud around the *Baron*.

Jeb checks his watch. The barge is right above them. That gives him another ten to fifteen minutes to search for the crates. He hopes they are still entombed in the wreckage. He runs his hands across the river bottom. If he has to do any digging, he isn't sure he will have time. He motions for Margaret to help him move the silts and clays that have covered the ancient vessel. As he pushes the sediments away, they drift up from the bottom and cloud the area in front of his face.

The seconds tick by as they sift through the fine-grained material. After five minutes of digging, they haven't found a board or anything associated with the *Baron*. Jeb searches frantically as time speeds away. Margaret shakes her head, arms elbow-deep in the river bottom. The brightness of her eyes has dimmed. Maybe they are in the wrong spot. It is difficult finding the actual spot when you're in a muddy river looking for something that has been hidden for so long. Jeb feels the desperation building inside him and he along with Margaret are on the verge of giving up on this area of the river.

The rumble in the sediments starts to dissipate. Jeb checks his watch quickly. After the barge passes, their cover will be gone. Jeb had hoped to have the crate out of the water before that took place, but it looks like he will be down here a little longer. Jeb floats above the remnants of the *Baron* and looks from the paddle wheel to the front portion of the boat. The boat's final resting place has it pointing downstream. What if the crates were dislodged by the current, and instead of being in the center, maybe they were pushed toward the bow?

He swims downstream, and as he moves, he submerges his hands in the sediments. He fingers brush against something solid. His heart jumps as he feels the smooth, linear texture. Jeb digs frantically, throwing the sediments into the swift current. As he digs around the wooden object, he locates an angular corner. Jeb scrapes away the last bits of silt and clay, and he is staring at a perfectly preserved wooden box.

Margaret swims beside him, and the glow from her spotlight illuminates the crate. The sediments drift slowly around them as Jeb grabs the rope handles and pulls with all his strength. The crate breaks free from its watery tomb, and he places it at his feet. Margaret slowly rubs her fingers on the surface. She pulls the lid from the crate and slowly lifts the box top.

Jeb's breath catches in his chest as the bright light reflects off the gold coins hidden inside. *That is a lot of gold*, Jeb thinks as he smiles. Margaret hurriedly places the top on the box and digs enthusiastically in the mud beside the resting place of the first crate. She pulls up handful after handful of the light-brown material. Jeb thrust his hands into the soft material and pulls the thick clay and collected silts away from the bottom.

His fingers graze across another wooden crate. Jeb points excitedly, and Margaret rushes over to help. Together, they remove the remaining material, and there in front of them is a box that is black and appears charred. Margaret grabs one side, and Jeb grabs the other, and they hoist the crate from the thick mud.

The box is light and easy to maneuver. They place the blackened crate beside the box filled with gold, and Margaret reaches out a shaking hand and grabs the lid. She slowly pulls the lid upward, and inside the box are four glistening metallic spheres. Jeb stares in disbelief—the spheres are glowing and revolving emitting a low level hum as they move. He has never seen anything like this in his life. They move in an elliptical pattern in the box, but they never collide. It seems a force is keeping them from touching.

Jeb reaches his hand toward the metal, and he can feel an energy pulsing through the water. Before his hand can touch the metal, Margaret quickly grabs his hand and pulls it from the box. She drops his hand and places the top securely on the crate. She points to the box and then points to the surface. Jeb grabs the crate filled with the gold, and Margaret grabs the crate filled with the pulsating metallic spheres.

They point their bodies toward the surface and kick off from the *Baron*. The crate of gold is heavy, but the water helps Jeb carry the contents. He checks his air supply, and he doesn't have much air left. The frantic searching must have caused him to use too much air. Jeb takes short gasps as the last bits of air trickle from the tank.

This isn't good, he breathes as he kicks wildly toward the surface. Margaret is above him, moving easier through the muddy water. Jeb's chest burns as the air runs dry. He bites on the mouthpiece and pushes his legs harder. Above him, Margaret breaks the surface of the river and paddles toward the shore. Jeb bursts through the surface of the water and spits the regulator out of his mouth, taking in deep gulps of welcome air.

After a few gulps, he follows Margaret toward the shore. Clem wades in and helps Margaret pull the crate from the water. He delicately places the black crate on the ground and touches the lid.

Margaret speeds out of the water and knocks his hand from the box. "I wouldn't do that if I were you," Margaret hisses.

Clem's eyes narrow as he rubs his hand.

Jeb struggles with the second crate as he

brings the rectangular box out of the water. Clem hurries into the water and grabs the handle on the opposite side. He licks his lips as he eyes the giant chest. "Is this the gold?" Clem says, grunting under the weight. "Man, there has to be a hundred pounds or more," Clem continues. His eyes are bright, and he pulls the box frantically toward the shore.

Jeb and Clem delicately place the crate on the ground. Jeb falls to his knees and takes in a few deep breaths of fresh air.

"Are there any others down there?" Clem mutters.

Jeb nods his head as he wipes the water dripping onto his face from his wet hair.

"Shouldn't we go get them?" Clem asks.

Jeb shakes his head. He points downstream toward the retreating barge and towboat. The boat is a hundred yards downstream and disappearing around a bend in the river. "Our cover is gone," Jeb says, out of breath. "We need to get what we brought up out of here before the bad guys show up. We can get the rest another night."

Clem jumps excitedly, grabbing the end of the box. "Let's go," Clem says hurriedly. He watches Jeb with his mouth hanging open as Jeb wiggles out of his tank harness.

"Give me a second," Jeb bristles. Jeb drops the empty tank in the sand and pulls the flippers from his feet.

CHAPTER 12

Contents Revealed

J eb slowly climbs to his feet and grabs the crate. He lifts with a huff and waddles toward the tree line. Jeb turns and catches site of Margaret. She is sitting beside the light-weight box with the metallic spheres hidden inside. "You ready?" Jeb calls softly.

Before she can answer, the stillness of the night is shattered. The roar of engines reverberates from the stone faces of the gorge walls. Up the river, four speed boats race toward them. Jeb knows the person in the lead boat. He can see long hair blowing in the current of air. "Margaret, it's time to go!" Jeb screams as he pulls the heavy gold-filled box toward the safety of the trees.

Margaret jumps to her feet and lifts her crate with ease. It looks weightless in her hands, and she rushes into the thick privet.

Bright searchlights sweep across the beach in front of them, and Jeb stumbles and falls into the sand. Clem pulls on the crate, forcing Jeb back to his feet. As they make it to the tree line, one of the spotlights hits Jeb. They have been seen. There is no way for them to trek back to the car carrying all the loot. Jeb and Clem rush through the thicket, and the branches scratch Jeb's face and arms. Warm beads of blood rush to the surface on the fresh cuts.

"We know you're in there!" Long Hair yells boisterously from the boat. The spotlight moves from side to side at the point where Jeb entered the trees. The yellow light filters through the foliage and reflects off his watch. Long Hair laughs loudly. "I thought you would have learned by now, but evidently not."

Jeb looks toward Margaret. Her green eyes are piercing as she glares back. "He's not getting this," she whispers.

Jeb nods slowly and looks through the privet. Long Hair is standing behind the wheel of a speed boat, his automatic rifle pointing toward them. A sneer stretches across his face. "Last chance," Long Hair says.

Clem grabs Jeb's arm. Clem's eyes are wide, and he is shaking. Jeb knows that look. That is the look of "Why did I listen to you again? We go for treasure, and we end up getting shot at." Jeb is starting to agree with him. The last two adventures have been very difficult. When he started treasure hunting, Jeb had an idea that it would be glamorous and exciting trying to decipher clues hidden in the past. The thrill of finding long-lost treasure and never telling anyone about it seemed perfect. No one told him that hunting for lost gold was going to be deadly.

Jeb looks toward Margaret, and she is crawling backward slowly, pulling the box with her. Her movements cause small rustles in the leaves, and Long Hair turns toward the sound. "Time's up," Long Hair says.

Suddenly, fire erupts from the end of the rifle, and bullets rip through the leaves of the trees. Fragments of green and bits of bark rain down upon them as he sprays the area above them with a hail of bullets.

Jeb's heart beats violently, and the air is thick, making his breath short and labored. He turns and sees Margaret lying over the box as if she is protecting it. "Oh no," Jeb says silently.

She isn't moving.

Jeb fears she has been hit by the gunfire. Jeb looks at Clem, and he is whimpering beside Jeb, pressed into the ground. Jeb grits his teeth. "All right!" he yells.

Long Hair smiles as he unleashes another round of bullets into the trees above Jeb's head.

"*All right!*" Jeb yells louder.

Jeb keeps his eyed focused on Long Hair, and Long Hair lowers the barrel of the automatic rifle and motions toward the other boats. Jeb can't see the others, but he hears splashes in the water upstream and downstream. A few seconds later, armed men burst through the trees and surround them. Jeb smiles as he raises his arms high into the air. "Nice of you guys to drop by," Jeb says, smiling, "It was going to be difficult getting these boxes back to the car, but since you're here, can you get this end?"

A man with large muscles carrying a rifle that appears too small in his big hands smashes the stock of the gun into Jeb's stomach.

Jeb falls to his knees. "Why did you have to go and do a thing like that?" Jeb wheezes.

The man raises the gun for another strike.

"That's enough," Long Hair says slowly.

The burly man lowers his weapon.

Jeb pushes away from the ground and stands. He glares at Long Hair as the man pushes through the thick foliage. The bright spotlights from the boats cast everything around Jeb in a vibrant yellow glow. Long Hair stands over Clem, looking down at his lifeless body. He kicks Clem savagely in the ribs and the *thud* of his boot against Clem's body is deep. Clem groans. "Looks like we got a live one." Long Hair laughs. "Not much of a hero, though."

The men around Long Hair laugh.

Long Hair slowly walks toward Margaret. She is still gripping the box in her arms, and she remains lifeless. Long Hair stands above her, and he looks from Margaret to Jeb. A sneer spreads across his face as he reaches and grabs a handful of her hair. "What have we here?" Long Hair chuckles as he pulls.

Margaret is lifted from the ground, and her lifeless form hangs limply in his hand. Long Hair looks at her face, and the sneer fades quickly. "Oh my," he says and drops her to the ground. She crumbles in a heap beside the box.

Long Hair rubs his chin with his left hand as he stares at her. "Unexpected. Quite unexpected," Long Hair mutters. He motions toward the other men. "Get them on their feet," he barks. "And get them to the boat."

The muscular man strikes Jeb's stomach with the barrel of the gun. Jeb holds on to his midsection as he gasps for breath. Instantly, Jeb is pulled upright by his hair The muscular assailant laughs as he drags Jeb into the shallow water. "You're not going to like this at all," he says joyfully as he pulls Jeb toward the boat.

Long Hair jumps onto the speedboat and grabs the radio handset. It is a satellite phone with a long antenna. It looks military-issue, which would make sense. Jeb believes these guys are FBI, NSA or CIA. "Boss, we have them," Long Hair growls. "The package looks to be intact, as well." Long Hair nods as the other men bring Clem and Margaret toward the boat.

Two other soldiers carry the crate filled with gold and place it on the shore in front of the boat. A man wearing a backward baseball cap carefully creeps through the privet, carrying the box with the shining, rotating spheres. Jeb watches how carefully the man is with the cargo.

"Be careful with that!" Long Hair yells as the man delicately places it next to the crate filled with the gold.

Jeb is watching intently when he is hit between the shoulder blades with the end of a rifle. He falls forward into the packed sand of the beach. He glares at the smiling muscular guard. The guard shrugs his massive shoulders and stands over him. They drop Clem beside Jeb, and Margaret is tossed onto the ground beside them.

Jeb tries to see if she was hit by the gunfire, but he doesn't see any blood. Her chest rises and falls slowly. *At least she is alive*, he thinks as he looks at Clem. "You okay?"

Clem lifts his head from the sand, and blood is running over his right eye from a cut on his forehead. "What do *you* think?" he says as he spits blood onto the sand.

Jeb grits his teeth and watches Long Hair.

"She is here, and she has the box," Long Hair says into the handset. He nods slowly. "You want me to take care of them?" Long Hair asks into the phone. He nods again and places the handheld beside the wheel. "She's coming with us," Long Hair says to the soldiers. "Get the crates on board."

Long Hair jumps from the boat into the water and strides toward Jeb with a sneer on his pointy face. "You were oh so close," Long Hair jeers. "But just like every time in the past, we win." He grabs a fistful of Jeb's hair and pulls Jeb upward. His face is inches from Jeb's, and Jeb can smell the staleness of his breath as he exhales.

"Unfortunately, your time has come to an

end." Long Hair sneers. "You are no longer needed." Long Hair strikes Jeb in the mouth with a quick jab that sends his head backward.

Jeb glares at the man as he wipes the blood from his mouth. "You're going to pay for that," Jeb spits.

Long Hair laughs.

Jeb shoots to his feet, steaking toward Long Hair. He thrusts his shoulder into the midsection of Long Hair. Jeb wraps his arms around the man's skinny waist and drives Long Hair to the ground. The rifle flies into the air, and Long Hair groans under Jeb's weight. Jeb grabs his long hair and violently shoves his head underwater. Long Hair flails his arms and rolls his shoulders, trying to free himself from Jeb's grasp.

"I said you were going to pay," Jeb growls as he pushes his knee into Long Hair's back.

"Hey!" The muscular soldier yells as he points his rifle at Jeb.

Jeb rolls his knee from Long Hair's back and pulls him upright. Long Hair sputters and sags, but Jeb keeps his body behind Long Hair's. The five soldiers move toward him as Jeb backs into the boat. All of the men have their weapons trained on him, and if he moves out from the cover, they will surely shoot him.

Finally, Long Hair speaks with a caustic, sneering voice, "You don't know who that is, do you?" he growls, pointing toward Margaret.

Jeb watches as Margaret inches toward the

crate. "Yeah," Jeb says, "I know who she is."

Long Hair laughs. "She once worked for us. Did she tell you that? That is why the boss wants her alive."

Jeb and Margaret's eyes meet. Her eyes sparkle in the floodlights from the boat. She swiftly grabs the handle and quietly pulls the crate toward her.

"It was her job to protect the weapon," Long Hair continues. "And here she is, using you to take it for herself." Long Hair shakes his head. "So gullible."

Margaret pulls the crate slowly backward, keeping her eyes on Jeb. He isn't sure what she is doing as she inches backward.

Jeb's mind is working quickly as the soldiers move around him, trying to get a clean shot.

"What would you say if me and my friend leave? You can have both boxes," Jeb says firmly.

The muscular soldier laughs, and Long Hair strains to look at him. "Sorry to say, but no deal," Long Hair says.

Jeb thinks about yelling that Margaret is getting away and letting her and the soldiers fight it out, but he can't do it.

"You're going to die, and just like old Captain Scotty, nobody will ever find you." Long Hair rolls his shoulders and plants his feet on a rock in the riverbed. He throws Jeb over his shoulder.

Jeb lands with a splash in the cold river. His arms and legs scrape against the abrasive sand, causing them to burn. Jeb shakes his head, trying to clear the throbbing feeling. As he looks up, the muscular soldier and Long Hair race toward him. Two of the other men sprint in Margaret's direction, guns drawn.

Long Hair and the muscular soldier stand over Jeb with their weapons drawn. "This is where it ends," Long Hair says with a smile as he places his finger on the trigger.

Jeb glances at Margaret, and she gives him a half smile as she pulls the lid from the box. Her eyes sparkle brightly in the glow of the floodlights as the metallic spheres shoot into the air and rush rapidly in circular patterns over everyone's heads.

Jeb's eyes are trained on the rotating and pulsating orbs as they move in synchronized patterns over the beach. They first move in parallel straight lines, then they form wide, looping figure-eights. The motion causes the air to become thicker around Jeb, and his breath catches in his throat. His chest is tight, like someone is sitting on his ribcage. Jeb's ears start to pulse and burn as if he is sitting at the bottom of the river.

The metallic spheres grow brighter and brighter with each passing second and begin to rotate around each other with such speed that they appear like thin streaks of light in the sky. The pressure inside the rotating vortex the spheres are creating is excruciating. Jeb rolls out of the water, holding his ears tightly in his hands. It feels like the air is being yanked violently from his heaving chest.

Through the pain, Jeb looks through narrowed eyes. Long Hair and the muscular soldier are on their knees, gazing upward with wide eyes at the spinning balls of light. Tiny tears of blood flow downward from their eyes as a high-pitch humming sound emanates from the air around them.

It feels like the air is going to rip apart into atoms. The pressure around Jeb builds. He isn't sure how much more he can endure before he passes out —or dies. He grits his teeth tightly and presses his hands firmly against his ears, hoping the event will end soon.

Jeb isn't sure what is happening, and it feels like his mind is slowly drifting away from his body. He has never experienced a force of this ferocity in his life. As a student studying structural engineering, he never heard of anything like this occurring. Jeb guesses the forces the vortex generates are equivalent to forces exerted on a cornerstone of a building. At this moment, he is the cornerstone.

Jeb looks through his squinting eyes toward Margaret. He hopes she is faring better than he is at the moment. The air around her is blurry, and it pulses. She is sitting on her knees with the box directly in front of her. Her hands are lying on her thighs, and her gaze is penetrating as she looks at him. Margaret doesn't blink as the air flashes in brilliant red-and-green colors. It is like being inside a lightning storm.

Jeb can't look away. He is entranced by the bright flashes of color and the deafening hum filling the air. The funny thing is, Margaret seems to be immune from the violence of the storm. She doesn't have her hands over her ears. Her eyes aren't bleeding. The great pressure filling the air and the high frequency sounds do not faze her. Jeb is perplexed, and this is something he will need answered if they ever make it off this beach.

Jeb's eyes burn uncontrollably, blurring the image of Margaret. He catches a sudden movement to his right, and as his eyes follow the motion, the muscular soldier falls to the ground. Jeb stares into the man's face—his bulging eyes and protruding tongue look grotesque. *One less to worry about*, Jeb thinks as the pressure inside his head mounts. It feels like an elephant is standing on his face, threatening to push his brain out his ears.

The world spins around him, and Jeb feels the contents of his stomach moving upward, burning the lining of his esophagus. The acid is caustic, and it burns into his throat and nasal cavity. Jeb's eyes bulge. He closes them tightly. He doesn't want to look like the dead soldier beside him.

The humming amplifies and intensifies into a violent rush. The air compresses Jeb, and it feels like a crate of bricks is resting on his chest. As Jeb takes a labored breath, the air burns his lungs and he swallows hard. *This is it*, Jeb thinks. *This is the last breath I get to take. At least it is on the river*. Blackness envelopes him, and the piercing hum from the air reaches a crescendo.

Instantly, the humming stops and the pressure is lifted. Jeb opens his eyes slowly, and as he looks into the sky, small rings of light move in his vision and disappear. The metallic spheres are moving slowly in zigzag patterns. Jeb follows their path, and he can see the reflective surface. The water and the trees along the river are visible on the edges of the metal balls.

He watches the balls slow and then race toward the box. Jeb blinks twice, making sure his eyes aren't playing tricks on him. The metallic spheres hover over the box and slowly descend into the wooden crate. There is silence along the river. There is no sound from the flowing water or the swaying trees.

Jeb crawls toward Margaret on the shore. She delicately places the top on the box and keeps her hands resting on the weathered wood. Jeb feels like he is moving in slow motion as he forces one hand over the other. His legs are weak, and the muscles in his arms twitch with each motion. He looks around slowly and sees the military men lying on the beach, unmoving. He turns, searching for Long Hair, and sees the man floating face-down in the slow-moving water.

That is one less thing to worry about, Jeb thinks as he claws his way onto the sandy shore. His arms tremble as he looks along the beach. Clem is lying on his stomach, his body rising and falling with each breath. Jeb crawls slowly and falls onto the beach beside Margaret. He looks up at her. "What happened?" Jeb says, breathing heavily.

Margaret shrugs her shoulders. "Not sure

what you mean," Margaret replies.

Jeb rolls onto his back and stares at the starlit sky. His arms and legs are heavy, but he smiles. "I'm just going to lie here for a few minutes, then you are going to tell me how all this happened," Jeb says slowly.

Margaret shakes her head. "I don't think that would be wise," she responds coldly.

Jeb's ears ring, and he grits his teeth. "Look, lady," Jeb growls, "I just witnessed magic metallic spheres dancing through the sky, causing a vortex or a whirlwind—I'm not sure which. And it caused these strong, healthy guys to drop dead."

"And you think knowing will help you explain when people ask?" Margaret replies.

"I'm not talking about what happened here ever again," Jeb says, closing his tired eyes.

"Because people wouldn't believe you?"

"Yep. I don't want to sound like a raving lunatic."

Margaret touches his shoulder, and he can feel the energy pulsing through her fingers. That is another question he could ask, but he decides against it. "I want to know for the sake of knowledge. What did I risk my life for?" Jeb says.

Margaret squeezes his shoulder. "For the gold, of course." Her voice is soothing, and it sounds like she is speaking in the rhythm of a song.

Jeb feels his body becoming lighter, and all he can hear is her soothing voice. He is at peace, and as the wind rustles through the trees, he drifts into a deep and content sleep.

*****

Jeb opens his eyes slowly, and the first rays of sunlight fill the pearly blue sky with streaks of orange and yellow. He rubs his face and slowly turns his head. Jeb is sitting in the driver's seat of his Saab. He turns, and Clem is sleeping in the passenger's seat. How did he get here? Jeb grabs the door handle and opens the door slowly. The humid morning air strikes his face as he rolls from the car.

Jeb moves lethargically around the car with his wetsuit rubbing against his skin. His legs feel heavy, like he is wearing a huge set of ankle weights. He stumbles to the rear and places his hands on the trunk. He takes a deep, labored breath. What happened? The last thing Jeb remembers is being in the center of a spinning vortex and the bad guys falling over dead. His head starts pounding as he leans against the car.

Where is Margaret? Jeb hits the side of his head with his palm, trying to shake the memories free. She was with them. Where did she go? Jeb pushes away from the car and stumbles along the trail to the river. He needs to see what happened. His head throbs, and there is slight buzzing in his ears. Jeb forces his way through the branches of the trees and the thick undergrowth.

Finally, he sees the river through the gaps in the privet and pine. He stops abruptly. The river is empty. He races onto the shore and looks upstream and downstream. Nothing. An eagle soars high overhead on the updrafts coming from the river. Jeb falls to the ground and buries his head in his hands.

It is like nothing happened here last night. The four boats are gone, along with the men and their weapons. Jeb struggles to make sense of what isn't here. He stands and walks along the beach, looking for any evidence they had been there the previous night. The sand is smooth, and it appears it has been raked flat. Someone doesn't want there to be a trace of evidence.

After searching for twenty minutes along the shore and in the thick undergrowth, Jeb walks along the forest path toward the car. It gives him time to think. The humming in his ears stops, and the throbbing has subsided. *It had to be Margaret.*

How did she get four boats and all the bodies carried away before morning? How did she sweep away all evidence of their encounter last night? Those questions gnaw at him all the way back to the car. What were the shining spheres that shot into the sky and killed all those men? Why didn't the spheres kill *him*?

There are lots of questions but very few answers.

The heat of the morning increases as the sun shines down from the peak of the ridge. Jeb opens the door to his Saab and climbs inside. The keys are in the ignition, and he turns the car on. Cold air blows from the vent, filling the car with welcome relief from the stifling humid air outside.

Jeb taps Clem on the shoulder repeatedly. "Hey. Wake up," Jeb presses. He pushes on Clem's shoulder again. "*Hey*. You awake?"

Clem grumbles and swats at Jeb's hand.

"Good to see you're well," Jeb says. "I'm not sure how she got you into that seat, though."

"What are you talking about?" Clem grumbles tiredly.

"Do you remember anything about last night?" Jeb asks.

Clem opens his eyes, and they dart around the cabin wildly.

"Hey, calm down. Everything is fine," Jeb says.

Clem sits rigidly upright and looks out the window. "How did I get here?" he says frantically. "Where are those guys?"

Jeb claps Clem on the shoulder. "Those are good questions, but unfortunately I don't have any answers to them."

Clem settles into the seat and closes his eyes.

"I guess we should get out of here," Jeb says, looking out at the quiet forest.

Clem pinches the bridge of his nose. "What happened to the woman?"

Jeb shakes his head slowly. "Not sure."

Clem grabs the door handle and throws the door open. He swings his feet out of the car onto the roadway. "Don't call me again," Clem says as he stands up. His legs wobble, and he grabs the open door to steady himself. "Finding treasure isn't worth it," Clem growls. He slams the door and walks toward his truck.

Clem doesn't look back, and Jeb doesn't blame him. That is the third near-death experience they have had in the last few weeks. That has an impact on you. Jeb watches Clem climb into the truck. The engine comes to life, and the tires spin in the dirt, sending brown clouds of smoke into the air. As the tires catch, Clem speeds away.

Jeb puts the car in drive and moves leisurely down the trail. He is lost in thought as he pulls onto Highway 41. He presses on the accelerator, and the car whines as it moves through the gears. At this rate, he will be home in Camden in less than an hour. Jeb thinks about jumping on his paddleboard and going for a nice cruise along the river when he gets home.

CHAPTER 13

Crate of Gold

J eb parks the car in the gravel lot of the marina. It feels good to be home, and he throws the door open and jumps out onto the shifting gravel. He walks to the rear of the car and opens the trunk. His mouth falls open as he stares at the contents inside. There in front of him is the crate he pulled from the bottom of the river. The cargo from the Baron.

Jeb's mouth is dry, and he looks around the car cautiously. He reaches toward the box, hands trembling. His fingers touch the smooth wooden crate, and he slowly opens it. He leans his head close, and he sees the gold glow from the contents. He whistles as he places the top on the box. She placed the gold in the trunk. Jeb looks around the car again, making sure no one is watching.

Jeb grabs the crate and lifts. It seems lighter than it was last night. He carries the box across the gravel lot onto the gangplank. Calvin stands on the alleyway, spraying water onto his boat. He looks at Jeb as he moves by. "What you got there?" Calvin says, squinting his eyes.

Jeb smiles. "An antique wooden box," Jeb says, winking.

"Ah," Calvin replies. "I suppose that box is what kept you out all night."

Jeb nods as he places the heavy crate on the wooden planking of the gangway. "A treasure hunter's job is never done." Jeb laughs.

"Good to have you home, son," Calvin replies.

"It's good to be home," Jeb says with his foot on the box.

A soft breeze blows through the slips in the marina. The motion of the air is cool against Jeb's sweat-drenched skin. The boats rock on the waves of the water caused by the blowing air. Jeb hops from the railing onto the deck of his boat. He pulls the heavy box on board and sits on the top.

Jeb watches a long barge drift down the river. The one from yesterday helped him extract this sizeable amount of gold he is sitting on. He smiles as the towboat blows its deep, resonating horn. Jeb slowly gets to his feet and opens the front door. He holds the door open as he pulls the heavy crate into the dark living room.

He flips on the light, and the room is filled with pale fluorescent light. Jeb drops the handle of the crate. "I thought I might see you again," Jeb says, smiling as he walks to his chair.

Margaret is sitting on the couch wearing black pants and a white button-down shirt. Her short hair falls down around her pearly white face.

"Thought I would thank you before I got out of here," Margaret says sternly.

Jeb sits and stares at her still-calculating face. "I don't think you needed me to find the wreck," Jeb says, shaking his head.

Margaret studies Jeb silently for a few seconds, then she looks away. "I needed you to find the spot," Margaret replies distantly. "I knew it was in the river. I didn't know where. That is where your expertise was needed."

"You could have done the survey," Jeb says, laughing.

Margaret shakes her head slowly. "That would have tipped off the wrong people."

Jeb grits his teeth. "So you let me take the heat," Jeb growls.

Margaret shrugs her shoulders. "It was the only way."

Jeb laughs loudly as he glares at her. "They could have killed me," Jeb snarls.

Margaret stands and walks slowly toward the window. She stares out, her back to Jeb. "That is the risk in endeavors such as this one," Margaret replies coldly.

"You never cease to amaze me," Jeb says, shaking his head. "You fed me all the information. You gave me the journal so I would know there was more to the Armstrong story." Jeb glares at her. The muscles in his jaw pulse and he grinds his teeth. "You used me," Jeb spits.

Margaret turns. "You wanted Grant's gold. That is the only reason you helped. So it seems you are just as selfish as I am," Margaret replies sternly.

Jeb stands and walks toward the galley kitchen. He grabs a glass and fills it with water from the tap. "Where did all the bodies go?" Jeb says, looking into the clear water in the glass.

"A clean-up crew," Margaret replies, "It was quick and easy."

"You thought of everything," Jeb says, downing the entire glass of water.

"There were a few unexpected moments, but for the most part, all went according to plan."

"So what now?" Jeb asks.

Margaret turns, and her bright-green eyes shine. Her expression is cold. She walks toward the door. "I leave, and you get a crateful of treasure. Seems fair," Margaret says. She grabs the door handle and stands for a second. "It was a pleasure working with you, Mr. Strauss."

As she opens the door, Jeb strides toward her. "Wait. I have one more question!" Jeb yells.

Margaret opens the door slowly.

"What were those spheres for, and what are you going to do with them?" Jeb asks.

Margaret turns and studies his face. "You know I can't tell you that," Margaret says.

Jeb shakes his head. "After all of this, you have to give me something," Jeb replies.

Margaret smiles and turns back toward the door. "I will give you one hint. The rest, I am sure being the researcher you are, you can figure out for yourself," Margaret says. "The spheres channel the electrical energy flowing through Earth. The results, you have seen for yourself." Margaret turns quickly and walks out the door.

Jeb stands, leaning against the door frame. He watches her climb the gangway toward the parking lot. That is more than he thought he would get out of her. He smiles as he watches her get into her car and drive away. At least he has a crateful of gold. It tended to make a few near-death experiences worth it.

He walks onto the deck and sits in his Adirondack chair. Jeb leans back and watches the barges go downstream on the slow current of the Tennessee River. He could have a safe, secure job as an engineer, but he prefers the thrill of the hunt. Besides, he wouldn't meet people like Margaret designing structures.

Jeb picks up his paddleboard and drops it into the water. It is a beautiful day, and he wants to be out on the water. Jeb grabs his paddle and climbs over the railing. He stands firmly in the center of the board and paddles toward the channel. On a day like today, if he had a real job, he would be in the office. He smiles as he thrusts the paddle into the water and pushes out into the current.

He will always be a treasure hunter. There is no chance of him being anything else.

ACKNOWLEDGEMENT

I would like to thank my family for their support. Without them, Jeb Strauss would never have made it to the page. My Wife, Rebecca, was a constant advocate for this story, and she always said it was worth telling. My children, Rory and Garrett, have listened to the telling of Jeb's adventures. They are a wonderful audience. I would like to thank Jeffrey and Lauren for creating the book cover. They are talented students, and I am glad that I am their teacher. Finally, I would like to thank my editor, Angela B. Wade. Jeb Strauss would not have made it this far without your expertise.

ABOUT THE AUTHOR

John V. Suter

is an author and teacher that enjoys a good treasure hunt. He has written two other treasure hunting adventures. He lives on a farm in Sale Creek, Tennessee with his family.